LOYAL HEART

When Lucy's sister Angela was injured in a car crash, Lucy felt responsible for Angela's two small sons, at the moment left with their grandmother, who had no time for Angela. So when old Mrs. Carrick advertised for a Nanny for the boys, Lucy got the job, keeping quiet about her identity. But was it a wise move? It antagonised the children's formidable uncle, Fergus Carrick, and brought down on herself the jealous spite of Fergus's friend, Celia Grange.

Books by Mary Cummins
in the Linford Romance Library:

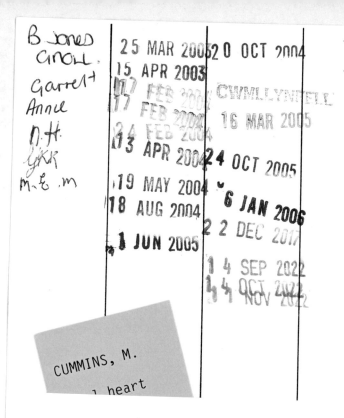

MARY CUMMINS

LOYAL HEART

Complete and Unabridged

LINFORD
Leicester

First published in Great Britain

First Linford Edition
published 2001

British Library CIP Data

Cummins, Mary
  Loyal heart.—Large print ed.—
Linford romance library
1. Love stories
2. Large type books
I. Title
823.9'14 [F]

ISBN 0–7089–9707–4

Published by
F. A. Thorpe (Publishing)
Anstey, Leicestershire

Set by Words & Graphics Ltd.
Anstey, Leicestershire
Printed and bound in Great Britain by
T. J. International Ltd., Padstow, Cornwall

This book is printed on acid-free paper

It had been a long and tiring journey. Lucy Abbott had left the London train at Kilmarnock, travelling by local train to Newton Stephens. There she had hesitated, looking longingly at a waiting taxi. But money was going to be tight now, so she sighed and made for the bus station. Nanny Campbell's cottage was on the outskirts of the small country village of Glenbanks, and the bus service was quite good. No more than thirty minutes later she was in Nanny's soft welcoming arms.

'My poor bairn!' she cried, looking at Lucy's white face. 'You're fair beat. I've been counting the minutes since your wire came.'

'Sorry I couldn't let you know earlier, Nanny,' said Lucy, struggling in with her bags, which Nanny hastened to take from her.

'Well, you're here now, and I'm right glad to see you,' beamed the old woman, 'and not before time, by the look of you. The big city hasn't exactly put roses in your cheeks, and you look as if you wouldn't hurt for a few good meals. What the good doctor would say if he could see you now, I daren't think! He'd have a thing or two to say to me for not looking after you.'

She had settled Lucy on the settee in front of a blazing fire, though the weather was far from cold. Lucy leaned back in her chair, allowing the wash of Nanny's tongue to run over her like the clear fresh water of the sea lapping over limp seaweed.

'I've been my own mistress for two years, Nanny Campbell,' she smiled, 'so Father could hardly blame you if I've lost weight. I'm just lightly built, that's all.'

'We'll see,' said Nanny non-committally. 'Och, it's a while now since your father died, we know, but Newton Stephens still misses him. It's all this Clinic stuff now. Maybe we don't have so long to wait for a doctor, but you're in and out that quick, there's no time to talk to anybody.'

She'd drawn up a small table, now laden with food which had appeared almost magically, and began to pour thick black tea from an old brown teapot.

'Now, get some life into you, and tell Nanny why you've suddenly decided to take your holidays in early April. I thought that Dr Bennett of yours could ill afford to spare his receptionist at this time.'

'And you were right, Nanny,' said Lucy wearily, as she sipped her highly-sweetened tea. 'Dr Bennett wasn't at all pleased when I told him about Angela's letter. Nanny, it isn't a holiday. I . . . I've come back to Newton Stephens indefinitely, and I'm going to have to find a job, quick.'

Nanny's eyes grew wide with surprise. Lucy had always seemed so much in love with her work. And it couldn't be Dr Bennett, who was old enough to be her grandfather! But . . . Angela's letter!

'What had your sister to say this time?' demanded Nanny. 'She hasn't honoured me with a letter for many a month, yet she was fair fu' of Canada at one time. I used to hope it would be the making of her, even if she had to run off with Stuart Carrick in order to get there. Her twin boys will be lumps o' bairns now.'

Lucy nodded, and accepted the buttered scone pushed in front of her. She didn't feel very hungry, but she knew Nanny would be glad to see her eating.

'They're three now,' she nodded. 'It's because of them I've come home. I . . . I'll have to find a flat, and a job here, Nanny. Angela and Stuart have been injured in a car accident, and the boys are being flown home to Prestwick. They're being sent to the Carricks' at Newton Stephens, but Angela doesn't want Stuart's people to have them. Not . . . not after . . . what happened. She wants me to look after them for her.'

Nanny Campbell looked as though the wind had been blown out of her sails.

'The Carricks have more right to the bairns than you have, lovey,' she said slowly. 'Besides, it's far too much responsibility for a wee thing like you.'

Sudden tears stung Lucy's eyes, mainly due to fatigue, but she blinked them away.

'How can I let my nephews live in a house where their mother isn't welcome?' she asked chokily. 'Old Mr and Mrs Carrick were so nasty when Angela married Stuart . . . '

'Mr Carrick is dead now.'

'Yes, but Mrs Carrick is still alive . . . and Fergus. I haven't seen him since I was a child, and I probably wouldn't know him now. But I remember him as a hard, dour-faced young man.'

Nanny rose and re-filled the teapot

with water from an old, shiny black kettle.

'He's weel respectit in Newton Stephens,' she said slowly. 'The Carrick Bookshop is gie well-known. Mind you, I'm not weel acquainted with them. The Carricks are too kind o' big folk for the likes o' me.'

'And me,' said Lucy, rather bitterly. 'And Angela, come to that. She and Stuart ran away six years ago, and they've never acknowledged her yet as a daughter of the house. No doubt they'll fall over themselves to take wee David and Ian. They're both Carricks, after all. But why should they, Nanny Campbell?'

There was a note of anger in Lucy's young voice.

'I want nothing to do with the Carricks, for my sister's sake,' she said, her eyes flashing. 'I want to go and collect those two boys, and look after them myself. I have Angela's letter here, giving me their guardianship. I'm a good shorthand-typist, so surely I can get a job with enough salary to keep us. Besides, I have that bit of money Daddy left.'

'Ye'll not go spending that,' said Nanny sternly. 'No, Miss Lucy, if yer heart is set on it, and if . . . ' She paused, her eyes very thoughtful . . . 'If Fergus Carrick agrees to give the bairns to you, then you can all stay here. It will only be temporary, surely, till Angela is better.'

'Of course it will,' said Lucy, though there was a note of fear in her voice. She'd had little real news as to the extent of Angela's and Stuart's injuries. He had been driving the car, and no doubt it was a case of reckless driving, thought Lucy darkly. Judging by her sister's letters, her married life had not exactly been easy, and Lucy had the strong impression that her brother-in-law was an irresponsible man.

'Fergus Carrick had better not prevent me from taking the children,' she said proudly. 'And, Nanny, thank you a thousand times. I'll work so hard to pay you for looking after us . . . '

'None o' that, Miss Lucy,' said Nanny sternly. 'There will be no talk of payment. I'll be glad to tak' the bairns, and to have you to look after for a wee while. I only hope that is the best solution, though.'

Her tone was very thoughtful.

'What else could it be?' asked Lucy, her vivid blue eyes wide and innocent.

'What else?' asked Nanny dryly. 'We'll mak' better plans in the morning, lovey. I'll have to sort up the house if we're to have two wee boys in the place. My best ornaments will get locked away for a start!'

* * *

Lucy lay back and relaxed. Now that the burden was shared, she felt very tired. Again she let Nanny's voice wash over her soothingly. Things seemed better now, and for the first time since she received Angela's letter, she felt hopeful that everything would be all right. Having her nephews to look after might even be a lot of fun.

Next morning Lucy woke early after a more refreshing sleep than she'd had for years. For a moment she allowed her eyes to roam round the small attic bedroom with its sloping walls and pretty cretonne curtains. It was good to be home with Nanny Campbell.

Lucy had been twelve when her father died, just two years after her mother. Angela was then nineteen, but Nanny Campbell had considered them both 'just bairns' and had brought them home to Airlie Cottage after their large old house had been sold up. Angela hadn't liked the cottage, and had been restless and dissatisfied, but Lucy knew that was mainly due to the big upheaval in their lives. It hadn't been easy for her beautiful sister to adjust herself to such changed circumstances. Even a course on flower arranging and a job with one of the most exclusive shops in Newton Stephens hadn't helped, though it was there she had met Stuart Carrick.

Lucy had been too young to comprehend fully the gossip and scandal occasioned by her sister's elopement. She only knew, from her sister's letters in later years, that the Carricks had blamed her for influencing Stuart, and it had angered Lucy that they should adopt this attitude. Surely they should have been proud and happy to have anyone so young and lovely as part of the family.

She herself had never been invited to meet her new relatives by marriage. The Carricks owned a very old-established booksellers business, and when old Mr Carrick died it was left to Fergus to run the family business, he being only two years younger than Stuart.

'That will make him twenty-eight,' thought Lucy, and tried to conjure up a mental picture of the dour-looking dark young man who was Angela's brother-in-law. But she hadn't seen enough of any of the Carricks to remember them clearly. She shrank inwardly from the forthcoming interview with them, when she must assert herself and claim Angela's children so that they could be under her protection. A hard, rather ruthless business man, and an autocratic old lady of seventy, were hardly fit guardians for two little children.

The bedroom door opened gently and Nanny appeared with a tray.

'Oh, Nanny, you shouldn't,' said Lucy, struggling to sit up in bed. 'You're not to wait on me.'

'After that long journey, you'll be tired,' said Nanny Campbell firmly. 'Will you be going out, Miss Lucy, or will you be in for your dinner?'

'Going out,' said Lucy, with a sigh. 'The quicker I see the Carricks the better. The children were being flown in to Prestwick airport, so they'll likely be here by now.'

Nanny only nodded non-committally, and bustled out after drawing all the curtains.

Lucy attacked her breakfast with more appetite than she'd have believed possible. She wished there had been

11

further news about her sister in the morning mail, as she'd sent on Nanny's address to Angela as to where she could be contacted. The last news had been that both Angela and Stuart had injuries which would require hospital treatment for some time, but neither were on the danger list.

As Lucy dressed, her eyes fell on a small framed photograph of herself and Angela, taken shortly before their father died, and she picked it up, looking closely at the tall leggy schoolgirl she had been, and the beautiful young girl who had one slender arm round her waist. Tears stung her eyes, but she brushed them away impatiently. There was no time to think of past happy days. Today she must face the Carricks, but the happy memories and the love of her sister stiffened her resolve, and she lifted her small chin proudly. Even the lovely grey soft wool suit did little else but make her look like a wide-eyed pixie of a girl, with curly black hair and Irish blue eyes, and, not for the first time, Lucy wished she looked more like her lovely blonde sister. Then she picked up her bag and ran lightly downstairs. Looks didn't matter. It was one's own inner courage, and the sure knowledge of having right on one's side, which counted.

Nanny was appreciative of her appearance, however, when she finally pinned on a small stylish hat.

'That makes you look older, Miss Lucy,' she remarked, 'but I must say it gives you a bit of dash.'

'That's good,' said Lucy with satisfaction. 'I don't know when I'll be back, Nanny, but I expect to have the children with me.'

For the first time there was a relaxed smile on Nanny's face when the children were mentioned. She couldn't approve of this arrangement, and still felt that Lucy was far too young and delicate for such responsibility, but there was no doubt it would be nice to have bairns about the place again.

'All right, Miss Lucy,' she said,

beaming. 'I'll have everything ready for the wee loves here. Only mind your step with old Mrs Carrick. She's like an auld duchess, and fair likes her own way, though I believe Mr Fergus is weel liked in spite of his dour looks. I've heard he's a fair man with nothing to his discredit.'

'That's good,' said Lucy, drawing on her gloves, and glancing at the large old grandfather clock in the corner of the cosy living-room. She knew it would be exactly ten minutes fast, even before checking it with her watch. Nanny had a thing about clocks, always keeping them ten minutes ahead of time, reckoning that this kept her ahead of all her chores.

'Ye'll get a bus the noo,' she was told, as Nanny followed her glance. 'It's due in aboot two minutes.'

''Bye, then,' said Lucy, and impulsively kissed her cheek. 'It's lovely to be home again, Nanny.'

★   ★   ★

The Carricks lived in a fine old house on the outskirts of Newton Stephens. Lucy had often passed the attractive ornamental gates of High Crest, and had peered along the gravel drive, admiring the fine façade of the spacious but compact house, its ivy-covered walls and sash windows giving an air of cosy comfort.

Now her knees trembled a little as her neat little black shoes crunched over the gravel, and she breathed deeply to steady her fast-beating heart.

The bell shrilled loudly, and shortly afterwards an elderly woman in a black dress and old-fashioned white cap opened the door.

'Good morning,' said Lucy brightly. 'I'm Lucy Abbott, and I should very much like to see either Mr or Mrs Carrick . . . '

'It's Mrs Carrick,' said the woman, with a smile, as she invited her in. 'She said a young lady would be coming to see her, but I don't think she expectit ye quite so soon. I'll tell her ye're here,

15

Miss . . . er . . . Abbott? Will ye have a seat for a minute?'

Slightly mystified, Lucy sat down on a beautifully carved but rather uncomfortable chair in the dark airy hall. It was old-fashioned, but there was an air of peace about the place, and from somewhere upstairs she heard the faintest trill of childish laughter, and her heart leapt excitedly. So the children were here! How exciting to see her two nephews at last. She had to control the urge to leap to her feet and run up the broad, highly-polished stairs.

However, a moment later the housekeeper again padded along the hall.

'This way, Miss Abbott,' she said pleasantly. 'Mrs Carrick is in the wee morning room, and hopes you won't mind if she sees you there. We're having a grand early spring, but there's a nip in the air, and the morning room has a good blazing fire. Mrs Carrick feels the cold now she's getting on a bit.'

As she spoke, she had reached a large

mahogany-coloured door leading off the corridor.

'Here's the young lady, madam,' she said, ushering Lucy into a small, charmingly cosy room. The blazing fire was no exaggeration, and the room felt warm and inviting. It was only when Lucy met the stare of the autocratic-looking old woman sitting in a high-backed chair that she began to shiver again. How could she ever have considered herself a match for this elderly lady, so used to commanding attention, and having her own way, and who could dismiss her with only a glance? No wonder Angela had never become reconciled to her mother-in-law, thought Lucy, running a small pink tongue over her dry lips, and feeling as though everyone could surely hear the loud booming of her heart.

Then the hard old features softened into a smile, and Lucy gazed, astonished, as she was asked pleasantly to take a seat.

'Thank you, Nessie,' Mrs Carrick

said, as the housekeeper withdrew. 'Don't look so frightened, child. You're only being interviewed for a job. I've no wish to eat you.'

Piercing black eyes darted over her with a flash of humour in their depth.

'I told the High Street Agency I wanted a strong girl, since she'll have to cope with two obstreperous children. I said she'd have to be fond of children, too, and that these qualities were even more important than experience. I am concerned for my grandsons' welfare at the moment, since they're only three.'

Lucy felt as though she was living in some kind of dream.

'Er . . . there must be some mistake . . . ' she began.

'Why? Don't you feel strong enough to cope, Miss . . . er . . . Abbott? I must say I expected a more buxom young woman, but I suppose we of the older generation can't pick and choose these days. We have to take what we can get, and the Agency weren't even sure of sending anyone at all! At least you're clean and I've no doubt honest. I've another young girl, part-time, who'll help you wash them behind the ears for a night or two, but you'll be responsible for looking after them in general . . . seeing to their well-being and so on, Miss . . . er . . . er . . . ?'

'Abbott,' said Lucy, very clearly.

Surely she knew her daughter-in-law's maiden name! Surely that would give this autocratic old woman a clue as to who she was. Explanations were gradually becoming more and more difficult.

'Well?'

There was a sudden brisk steely hardening in the old woman's voice.

'W . . . well?' asked Lucy timidly.

'Make up your mind, Miss Abbott,' said Mrs Carrick testily. 'If you want to see the children, I'll have them brought down. No need to disturb them for girls who back out.'

Lucy's eyes lit up at the mention of the children.

'Yes, please,' she said, with enthusiasm, and there was a softening gleam in the piercing dark eyes.

'My son will want to take up references,' the old lady warned. 'I leave business arrangements to him. The Agency would tell you the salary. Satisfied with that . . . eh . . . EH?'

'Oh, ye . . . yes,' said Lucy hastily, then felt she could have bitten her tongue out. It was the first word she'd said which concealed her true identity. Now she had given the impression that she really was a girl being interviewed for a Nanny's job, and had made it practically impossible for her to give her true identity. What an effect this formidable old woman had on her! She felt completely tongue-tied, and the soft colour began to flood her cheeks.

A moment later, however, a sweet-faced country girl in a white apron and cap knocked on the door and ushered in two small plump boys as alike as peas in a pod. Both had Angela's soft shining fair curls and her firm dimpled chin, but their large solemn black eyes would one day snap and sparkle just like their grandmother's.

Lucy felt a lump rise in her throat, and had a wild impulse to open her arms and hug them to her, crying out that she was their Aunt Lucy. And even as they stared at her solemnly, she smiled through the film of mist over her eyes, then she bent down and did, in fact, hold out her arms.

The response was immediate, almost as though young Ian and David had recognized someone who belonged entirely to them. They rushed towards her and she held their soft warm bodies in her arms.

'Oh, you darlings,' she whispered huskily. 'You two little darlings.'

'Well, that seems to be a good testimonial,' drawled a deep voice from the doorway, and Lucy's sparkling blue eyes flew to meet the dark sardonic features of a tall thin man standing in the doorway. There was no need to wonder who he was, thought Lucy, as she looked at a much younger, masculine edition of the hard, determined old lady in front of her.

'Ah, Fergus!' said Mrs Carrick. 'This is Miss . . . Abbott. I'm afraid she's the only girl who has come from the Agency, but maybe she'll do.'

Her tone was slightly doubtful, and for the first time a spark of anger began to burn in Lucy. This . . . this old woman was discussing her as though she was a piece of furniture, without the dignity of her own personality. She felt reduced to the merest nonentity.

She stood up, a flag of colour in her cheeks, and drew a deep breath before telling them exactly who she was, and claiming the children for her own exclusive care. But as she glanced from the dark, aloof man to the gaunt, straight-backed old lady, she knew that she was no match for either of them, individually, and certainly not for the two of them together.

'What does Miss Abbott say?' asked Fergus Carrick, looking straight at her, and she was suddenly conscious that her hat had become crooked, and her clothes a trifle crumpled. For a moment she thought she detected a hint of laughter in the glittering black eyes.

'If . . . if you wish to offer me the job of looking after the children, I . . . I'll be happy to accept,' she said stumblingly.

'Splendid!' he approved. 'Can you start immediately? You'll be expected to live in, of course, but there are two rooms next to the nursery prepared for you. As I expect the Agency explained, this is only a temporary job, as the children's parents have met with an accident. Both are in hospital at the moment, in Canada.'

For a moment there was a crack in the cool, crisp voice, and Lucy caught the slight tremble of the old woman's lips, too, as she turned away and began to write on a fresh sheet of paper.

'Of course,' she nodded, and couldn't help adding, 'How . . . how are they?'

There was a hint of coolness in

Fergus Carrick's eyes as they swept over her consideringly.

'Making progress,' he said briefly, and she dropped her eyes to hide the sudden light of relief.

'As I say,' he continued briskly, 'you'll be required to live in, and the job is for an indefinite period of time, but hardly less than three months. Is that satisfactory?'

She nodded slowly.

'I would like to go and make some arrangements, then,' she said, thinking of Nanny Campbell. She would have to go back to Airlie Cottage and pick up her luggage, and make her explanations.

'This is a list of your duties,' said Mrs Carrick, with an aloof air now that the interview was almost at a close, and again Lucy felt like the smallest nonentity. 'You will be answerable to my son and myself, and have complete authority over the children. I would like them to have plenty of fresh air, and other things they need . . . orange

24

juice . . . cod liver oil.' She waved her hand airily. 'I shall want a report at regular intervals on their general well-being, and I shall also wish to see them every day.' She glanced at Lucy's address in front of her. 'Just one point . . . I see that your address is London. Have you any relatives in Newton Stephens?'

Lucy's mouth went dry, and her eyes flew to Fergus who was watching her intently.

'No,' she said, quietly and honestly. 'I . . . I used to live here many years ago. Now . . . now my parents have died, and I've come home again.'

'I see.' There was a faint softening to the grim face. 'Then you can return, with your luggage, in time for tea?'

Lucy nodded, and picked up her handbag, her legs feeling oddly shaky as she made for the door. Whatever was possessing her? she wondered crossly. Why in the world was she willing to live this lie? Why hadn't she the courage to tell the truth, and whatever would Nanny Campbell say? Then again a tinkle of childish voices came to her from an upstairs room, and she felt steadier. What did her own feelings matter? Wasn't this the best solution of all? As the children's Nanny, she would be able to take complete charge of Angela's children, and see to it that they didn't forget their mother while she was lying ill so many miles away. In this way she could look after them without quarrelling with the Carricks, and wouldn't have the worry of trying to find a job in order to keep them all.

But what would happen if the Carricks found out? she wondered, as her feet again crunched on the gravel, and her heart quailed at the thought of facing them in that event. They simply mustn't find out, she thought fiercely. At least, not until Angela and Stuart were quite better, and the children back again in the care of their parents. After that it wouldn't matter as she'd have no wish to see either of the Carricks again.

Yet Fergus Carrick's face was indelibly fixed in her mind, and his sardonic black eyes seemed to follow her all the way home. It was almost as if . . . as if . . . he knew already . . .

Nanny Campbell stared at Lucy as though she'd lost her wits.

'Have ye gone out of your mind, or something?' she demanded. 'I've never heard of anything so daft. Dae ye mean to tell me ye never let on who you are? Did they not even tumble to it when ye told them your name? Abbott?'

'It's a common enough name round here,' Lucy assured her.

'What aboot the Agency?' went on Nanny. 'What if they send a girl noo?'

'They won't,' said Lucy. 'I phoned them.'

But now that she was away from the influence of the Carricks, she felt a fool, and was willing to take whatever medicine Nanny dished out. How silly of her not to put the record straight right away. In fact, she ought to go right now and ring them up to explain things.

But she made no move. She sat quietly in the large leather chair by the fireside, looking with softened eyes at the two small stools Nanny must have retrieved from the attic. Nanny was going to miss sharing the children. Yet why should she? There would be plenty of opportunity to bring them here, openly and above board. She had sole charge of them, and a day out was quite permissible.

A small smile began to play about Lucy's lips. The Carricks, with their high-handed attitude to life and people, angered her. It might be rather fun to get the better of them. Fergus had said that Angela and Stuart might be better in about three months. It wasn't for ever, and she could surely keep up the pretence over that short period. It was just a matter of using her wits, and keeping her head.

'I think it's a good solution,' she said to Nanny firmly. 'It means that the

Carricks and I can share the children without dissention. It solves the job problem, too, and I'll have the children all to myself every day. I'll bring them over as often as I can, Nanny.'

'Yes . . . well . . . '

The old woman looked doubtful, then sighed. The younger generation were so energetic these days, and they often did daft-like things. She'd never have got off with such deception in her time.

Still, it might be the best solution. They were sure to find out the truth sooner or later, but by that time the Carricks would have come to know that Lucy was a different cup of tea from Angela.

Nanny's lips firmed as she remembered the older girl, who had been a pretty selfish young lady in her eyes. Lucy was worth two of her sister, but she'd been too young to see faults in Angela, and hadn't learned any since. Perhaps it was just as well that she'd never had her illusions destroyed. It gave her a childlike trust which was very appealing, though Nanny felt a sudden stab of fear as she looked at the young girl who seemed lost in her old armchair. She hoped no one would ever hurt her. Oh, she did hope so! Yet life could be very cruel at times, and some men could be cruel, even to those they loved. And sometimes especially to those they loved . . .

'Penny for them, Nanny,' grinned Lucy.

'Worth a lot more, Miss Lucy,' said Nanny, blushing a little. 'Now, mind ye come and see me whenever ye can. Surely they'll give ye time off. Bring the bairns . . . Oh, and if ye ever need me, just phone up the Post Office, and I'll be right up at High Crest in jig time.'

'Righto, Nanny,' said Lucy. 'I'll do that.'

* * *

But it was to be longer than she expected before she saw Nanny again.

Back at High Crest, Nessie Cree, the housekeeper, was waiting to take her up to her room. Lucy and Nessie had taken stock of one another, and liked what they saw. The housekeeper reminded her a little of Nanny Campbell, though Lucy felt they might have disapproved of one another. Nessie obviously loved to know everyone's business, and a good gossip was meat and drink to her.

Nanny Campbell confined her nosiness to members of the family and it was, in fact, only a form of concern for them. She would have thought it bad manners to 'spier' at folks the very way Nessie was 'spiering' now.

'It's a nice wee room,' she was saying, and Lucy wholeheartedly agreed with her. 'Er . . . is it yer aunt that lives here, you said?'

'No,' said Lucy, 'not my aunt. Does that door lead to the nursery?'

'Och no, that's a wee bathroom. That door over there opens out on to the nursery. There's bars on the windows, by the way, and central heating, so there won't be such a risk of fire. My, but them two wee boys have fair taken to you, Miss . . . er . . . '

'Abbott.'

Then Lucy softened, feeling that Nessie could do her no real harm. In fact, keeping her too much at arm's length might even arouse her curiosity further.

'It's Lucy,' she smiled. 'And I've no relatives here in Newton Stephens, though an old friend lives in a neighbouring village. My only relative is a sister, abroad,' she said, and managed to smile without batting an eyelid. 'But I love Newton Stephens. I'm glad I've come back.'

'Och, ye'll be happy here with us,' Nessie told her, the girl's apparent loneliness having caught at her heart. 'Old Mrs Carrick is a bit of a martinet, but if you do your work well, and give her no cause for complaint, she's very nice.'

She had taken Lucy's case and was

swiftly hanging away her clothes. From the nursery, she could hear the children laughing and knew that Rosie was still with them. She was a local girl, but only worked part-time, and after today she would go back to helping Nessie, but the girl didn't seem to mind.

'Mr Fergus, too, is very fair.'

The old woman's voice had softened and Lucy guessed how much she loved the young master, as she called him.

'He had thought at one time to be a lawyer only . . . Och, there I go, letting my tongue run away with me, and you'll be wanting to go to the children. That Rosie is too young for them, anyway. She's nobbut a bairn herself.'

A moment later Lucy was in the nursery, a long bright airy room which seemed perfect for the two small boys who ran up and down on soft slippered feet.

'Hello, Ian, hello, David,' called Lucy. 'I'll have to get to know which is which.'

Again the children came to her

obediently, and she bent to hug them.

'Hello.'

'That's David,' said Nessie, having banished Rosie to the kitchen. 'I know him because I put a blue shirt on him and a white one on Ian. I thought it would be a good way of telling them apart till we get to know them.'

'I'm Ian!' yelled the other boy, and Lucy could see which one was going to give her trouble. They aren't so very alike after all, she decided, looking more closely. Surely David was all Angela, whereas Ian . . . Ian was like a young Fergus.

'I'm Lucy,' she told them.

'Lu-cy,' repeated David, and Ian grinned and hugged her till her ears ached.

'Lu-cy,' he said.

★ ★ ★

Next morning Lucy presented the boys to their grandmother for her inspection at eleven, an interview at which she hoped to clarify a few details. She had checked their clothing, and had been appalled at its state. Many things needed mending, but were too cheap to be worthy of repair. She broached this tentatively, and watched the black eyes grow hard and glitter with anger. Her heart quailed, but a moment later she realized that the anger was not directed against her.

'I have no wish to discuss the children's background,' the old lady said crisply. 'Sufficient to say that their . . . the person in charge of them may not have been as . . . as . . . competent as one would wish.'

Lucy's apprehension turned to anger, and she almost gave herself away by rushing to defend Angela. How dare anyone criticize her sister! But already Mrs Carrick was opening a cheque-book on her desk, and writing with a firm, almost masculine hand.

'This ought to be sufficient for their temporary needs,' she said, handing it over. 'See to it that my grandsons are

36

suitably clothed for all weathers. Is there anything else, Miss Abbott?'

Lucy hesitated.

'No,' she said slowly, 'I think that's all. Except, perhaps, a check-up from your doctor. I noticed a small rash on David, and it looks like an allergy. He's perfectly fit otherwise.'

'I will ask Dr Steele to call.'

'I could always take them in to the surgery on the way past,' offered Lucy helpfully, remembering the days when her father was run off his feet.

'We are private patients,' Mrs Carrick told her coldly, then waved her hand rather indifferently. 'Oh, very well, if you wish, though I shall telephone so that you won't be kept waiting. I shall see the children again before bedtime.'

Suddenly, to Lucy's astonishment, the old lady looked down on the two chubby boys who were beginning to wrestle with each other on the carpet. She bent to separate them, but Mrs Carrick's long hard face had softened into a smile.

'Have you got a kiss for Grandmother?' she asked.

Immediately they flew to her, scram-
bling with scant ceremony on to her
hard, bony knees, and almost knocking
her carefully bound hair over her face.
She giggled like a girl while their strong
fat arms encircled her neck, then they
slid to the floor.

'Have a nice walk, my darlings,' she
said gently.

As they turned to go, Lucy could
hear Nessie talking to someone in the
hall, and a moment later the door flew
open and a girl stood there. Lucy
caught her breath with admiration and
surprise. The girl was tall, with
beautifully bound auburn hair, her
slender figure encased in a black
tailored suit, with a lovely fur stole
draped over her arm. This she handed
carelessly to Nessie. She looked straight
at Lucy, who stared again at the
perfectly-modelled face, marred by a
rather disdainful expression, and a hard
line to the mouth.

'Aunt Caroline, darling!' she gushed, carefully avoiding the boys as she stepped into the room.

'Good morning, Celia. These are my grandchildren and their governess, Miss Abbott,' said Mrs Carrick, rather proudly.

She motioned for Lucy to leave, and as she closed the door, she could hear the sharp voice replying, 'Well, darling, you could hardly expect me to be all over Stuart's children, could you . . . after what happened?'

What had happened, Lucy wondered curiously, and who was the beautiful girl? She'd called Mrs Carrick 'Aunt Caroline', so she must be some sort of niece.

Nessie was hovering around waiting for her.

'Would ye be better to have a wee drink of orange juice for the bairns before you go out?' she asked. 'And some coffee, maybe?'

'Oh, that would be lovely,' said Lucy gratefully. She and the children had their meals in the nursery, but now Nessie led the way into the kitchen.

'Rosie is oot at the shops,' the housekeeper told her, bustling about getting cups. 'I'll just carry this tray in for Madam and Miss Grange, then we'll have ours. There's the orange juice and biscuits for the boys, if you think you can manage that, Miss Abbott.'

'Just call me Lucy,' she smiled.

'All right, Miss Lucy,' beamed Nessie, picking up the fine old silver tray.

A moment later she was back, shaking her head a little.

'That Miss Celia is a right madam,' she said. 'She gets mair stuck up every day. Never a please or thank you.'

'Er . . . who is she . . . a niece of Mrs Carrick's?' asked Lucy.

'Devil a bit,' she was told. 'No relation at all. She was once engaged to Mr Stuart, the children's daddy, and now she's dangling after Mr Fergus. They can't shake her off, seein' as how Mr Stuart ditched her, so to speak. He ran off with another girl. Mind you, she was no great catch, but she can't be much worse than that Celia.'

She didn't notice the glint of anger in Lucy's eyes again. No great catch! No, a poor doctor's daughter *would* be no great catch to the Carricks.

'She was a bonny wee thing, wi' lovely fair curls, just like the bairns, but awfu' irresponsible.'

'Perhaps she was young,' said Lucy stiffly, and the housekeeper darted a look at her, seeing the offence on her face with surprise.

'Oh, aye, she was young enough,' she said, slowly, 'but she'd got her hooks into Mr Stuart all right. He did exactly what she told him. I've seen them together a few times, and he always waited on her every word. She was the ringleader when they ran away, nae doot aboot that. He was aye a softie.'

'Maybe . . . maybe he was only soft because he loved her,' said Lucy, her voice shaking. How she wished she'd

41

been open about who she was . . . but now it was too late! This was the only way she could keep in touch with the children now, and she would have to guard her tongue and feelings carefully. But it was hard when they spoke slightingly of her sister.

'I . . . I'm sorry,' she smiled to Nessie. 'It's just that . . . they're such nice children.'

'Aye, they're bonny,' the old housekeeper smiled, watching the two little boys drink their orange juice rather noisily. 'It's good to have bairns about the place again. It brings the old house to life, and Madam is like a two-year-old again.'

'You . . . you like Mrs Carrick?'

'Of coorse,' said Nessie. 'I've been here since I was a girl. Why would I stay if I didna like them? She's a hard-looking woman and likes her own way, but she's fair, and Mr Fergus is as fine a gentleman as breathed. Mr Stuart was a softie, but he wisna bad either. Poor young gentleman . . . all smashed up and lying in hospital, and the lassie, too.'

'Don't,' whispered Lucy, and was glad Nessie was too busy with the pots on the stove to see her white face.

'We'll go now, Nessie,' she said, rising. 'I'm ordering clothing for the boys, and calling in to see Dr Steele for a check-up for the boys. We should be back in good time for lunch.'

'All right, Miss Lucy. These two will be the better for some fresh air to run the mischief out of them,' she said, as the two little boys pushed and shoved each other out of the kitchen. They were going to have to learn discipline, thought Lucy, as she grabbed their hands firmly. And their manners left a lot to be desired.

★ ★ ★

It was fun shopping for the children, and Lucy enjoyed using her good taste, and striking a happy balance between what was practical and what was 'dressy'. She chose plenty of cotton T-shirts and pants, and was specially pleased with her purchase of bright scarlet macs and hoods, with gumboots to match. It rained a great deal in Newton Stephens and she did not believe in staying indoors because of the weather. The twins would still be taking their daily walk, if it came down in buckets.

Dr Steele's surgery was quite near High Crest and Lucy guided the children up the steps, and through the glass swing doors. A pretty receptionist looked up with a smile.

'You're just in time, Miss Abbott,' she said. 'Doctor has some calls to make soon.'

'Of course,' said Lucy, flushing because she'd forgotten the time.

The doctor who swung round from his desk was much younger than she'd imagined, and for a long moment they stared at each other. He was very fair, with pleasant boyish features and a wide smile. Lucy's dark curls had become windblown and there were flags of colour in her cheeks. She could see the sudden admiration in the young doctor's eyes, and coloured even more vividly.

'I . . . I'm sorry if I've kept you waiting,' she said huskily.

'Not at all, and you haven't.'

She liked his deep, pleasant voice, and sat down on the chair indicated. For once the boys were in awe of something or somebody, and stared back at Dr Steele stolidly. Lucy introduced them both.

'They've just come from Canada,' she told him. 'I'm in charge of them, and I would just like them to have a check-up. I don't know if they've had their inoculations or anything like that, and they both seem very well, but David has a small rash on his chest. I was wondering if it was an allergy.'

She unbuttoned the little boy's shirt, while Dr Steele examined him carefully, then turned him round, pressing his fingers into the back of his neck, then turning to examine Ian.

'I'm afraid it's more than an allergy,' he said, quietly. 'It's German measles. You'll have to keep the boys indoors for a few days. Luckily, it seems to be a mild form.'

'Oh dear,' gasped Lucy, 'and I've had them all over town. I should have listened to Mrs Carrick, and stayed in while you called to see them, only . . . well . . . my father was a doctor . . . '

She could have bitten her tongue out, but it was too late to recall the words, as recognition dawned in the young doctor's eyes.

'Dr Abbott! But of course,' he said, 'I remember him as a boy. I admired him very much.'

Lucy's face was scarlet. Perhaps Dr Steele didn't know that it was Dr Abbott's older daughter who had married Stuart Carrick, but if he mentioned Dr Abbott to Mrs Carrick, then Lucy's true identity would soon some out.

'Yes, I'm Lucy Abbott,' she said, quietly. 'Doctor, you . . . you'd do me a great favour by keeping this between ourselves. There . . . there are reasons why I don't want Mrs Carrick to know I'm Dr Abbott's daughter.'

Dr Steele's look became rather cool and impersonal.

'Of course,' he said crisply, 'your private affairs are no concern of mine. I'll call and see both children tomorrow. There's no need to confine them to bed unless they run a temperature.'

Lucy rose briskly to her feet, the colour again flooding her cheeks. She felt foolish at having had to ask Dr Steele to share a secret with her, and he was quite right to snub her. But it made her feel very small indeed.

Then he was smiling at her again, his brown eyes soft and gentle, so different from the hard black glitter with which Fergus regarded her.

'Good morning, Miss Abbott,' he said pleasantly. 'Until tomorrow, then.'

'Good morning,' she said breathlessly.

She arrived back at High Crest just as Fergus's car swung into the gravel drive, and he leapt out and raced up the steps to join them.

'Well, and how are my nephews today?' he asked, giving them all a piercing scrutiny. Lucy walked in front of him into the hall.

'Not . . . not so good,' she told him jerkily.

Why did he always make her feel so nervous? She stared up at him, wetting her lips, and was surprised to see a smile softening his face. How like his mother he is, she thought, looking at the thin, long features which could be compelling or forbidding.

'What's the matter?' he asked gently.

'German measles,' she said huskily. 'David had a rash and I thought it was an allergy, perhaps due to changes in his diet. But it's German measles. Ian is starting, too. I . . . I'm sorry.'

'Why?' he asked. 'You didn't give it to them, did you?'

She coloured with annoyance, feeling

like a small girl being laughed at.

'Of course not,' she said crisply.

'Then take them along to the nursery. I'll explain to my mother.'

'Oh, thank you,' she said gratefully, then turned with a start to see Miss Grange regarding them. She must have walked, unnoticed, out of Mrs Carrick's room, and was throwing on her lovely furs while regarding them curiously.

'Hello, darling,' she said huskily to Fergus, then turned to raise an eyebrow at Lucy.

'Come along, boys,' she said hurriedly. 'This way.'

'Odd little girl,' she could hear Celia Grange say, in her hard carrying voice. 'Sorry I can't stay to lunch, darling, but it's all fixed for the twentieth. Dinner at the Balmoral first of all, then we can go straight to the concert. *Everybody* will be there . . . '

★   ★   ★

The following evening Lucy was surprised when Nessie brought a message
inviting her to join Mrs Carrick and
Fergus for dinner. She received this
with mixed feelings, pleased to be
considered in this way, but apprehen-
sive of close questioning. Suppose she
gave herself away! It would be easy for
her unwittingly to answer a question
which would betray her relationship to
Angela.

However, it was more of a summons
than an invitation, and Lucy smiled her
thanks to Nessie, who promised to keep
an ear open for the boys, after they had
been put to bed. She turned her
attention to her wardrobe, and with
much thought, selected a very simple
dress in dark green silk, which made
her blue eyes shine like violets. Lucy
had earned a good salary in London,
and had indulged her one extravagance,
a taste for pretty clothes, to the full.
Now she studied her reflection with
quiet satisfaction, and decided she
would do. If only she could keep a

careful watch on her tongue, then she might enjoy an hour away from her new responsibilities.

She needn't have worried. As she walked downstairs, the high-pitched voice which was gradually becoming familiar to her floated up from the hall, and a moment later Lucy was again face to face with Miss Grange, who was very open to Fergus about her astonishment at seeing Lucy obviously about to join them.

'Why, Miss . . . er . . . Abbott,' she said, 'don't tell me Aunt Caroline has invited her to join us, Fergus darling. Surely she'd be bored with our conversation.' She turned away, linking arms with Fergus. 'I always think it's a mistake to invite a nursemaid to share a meal with the family,' she said, almost chidingly. 'It gives them quite the wrong ideas, darling.'

'Miss Abbott is not a nursemaid, Celia,' said Fergus, and for once threw an embarrassed glance towards Lucy, and held back, ushering both girls into the dining-room. Lucy's cheeks were colouring with anger, and her blue eyes sparkling like sapphires. She'd no idea that her inward anger made her blaze like a polished jewel, and drew Fergus's eyes to her, a sudden glint in their black depth.

But if this girl thought she could intimidate her, then she had another think coming, decided Lucy, her small chin lifting. Her black curls were close-cropped round her small head, and she acknowledged Mrs Carrick's presence deferentially and gracefully. The older woman looked from Lucy to Celia's beautiful petulant face. The older girl was elaborately dressed, and wore too many jewels for her age. There was an inscrutable expression on the old lady's face as they took their places at the large, highly-polished mahogany table, and Rosie began to help serve the meal.

'How is that marvellous new book by Duncan Strange going?' asked Celia, turning with animation to Fergus, and so obviously showing Lucy that she took a very personal interest in Carrick's. 'I expect you've ordered lots of copies. He's a real best-seller.'

'Not in Newton Stephens,' said Fergus quietly. 'We'll be lucky to sell what we have bought.'

'But, darling, don't you think that sometimes you could guide the tastes of your customers so much more? Newton Stephens is such a backwater in some ways. They can't see beyond Burns and Sir Walter Scott. They even think themselves daring if they buy Galsworthy or Bennett.'

Fergus laughed lightly, though Lucy caught a cool glint in his eyes. She suspected that he didn't like any criticism levelled towards Carrick's.

It was one of the oldest established booksellers in the West of Scotland, and in addition, carried a fine selection of paintings, beautiful glassware, and handsome leather goods. Their second-hand book department was also extremely well-known, and many people found their way to Newton Stephens, to browse round Carrick's and went home feeling uplifted by the time spent in the large old shop with the quiet peaceful atmosphere. Fergus knew his customers well, and knew how very wrong was Celia's assessment of them. They might still buy the classics, but modern novels, biographies and travel books were also very popular, though they preferred to judge books by their own standard, and not because it was smart to read some new author.

'Don't exaggerate, Celia,' he said teasingly. 'Anyway, Miss Abbott won't want to hear us talking shop.'

'Oh, I don't mind,' said Lucy quickly, glad to keep the conversation away from personal matters. She was fond of reading, and enjoyed a very mixed diet. 'I think I should find Carrick's quite fascinating.'

'And do you agree with Celia regarding the new Strange?' asked old Mrs Carrick unexpectedly. 'Do you think we're too much behind the times, and that we should influence our customers a great deal more?'

Lucy wriggled a trifle uncomfortably, disliking to be brought into the limelight and asked to express an opinion. She had plenty of opinions, but they weren't in keeping with her present circumstances, and she had no wish to cross swords with Celia Grange. Then she caught the other girl eyeing her scornfully, and again her small chin lifted.

'I prefer to think the customer is always right,' she said coolly. 'Mr . . . Fergus . . . will know exactly what to provide. That's part of his skill and his success. The public are not all fools who behave like sheep, buying books to leave around casually for effect. I'm sure most people who come to Carrick's buy books to read, and to enjoy.'

'If everyone thought like that, we'd still be reading penny dreadfuls,' said Celia, with a small superior laugh.

'I don't agree,' said Lucy quietly.

'Again I think the reading public have more taste and . . . and discernment than they get credit for. They'll soon show when they're bored with what is available, and a good bookseller, with his finger on the pulse as it were, will soon know what the trend is. Personally, I won't be buying the new Duncan Strange since by all accounts it's a follow-up to his last book. He has nothing to offer me.'

Both Mrs Carrick and Fergus were looking quite inscrutable, but Celia's eyes were sparkling dangerously.

'How unusual for a Nanny to be a book expert,' she purred softly, and Lucy bit her lip. She attacked her roast lamb without appetite, but she could sense the other girl's antagonism, and was glad when she and Fergus began to talk of local matters. She'd been too long away from Newton Stephens to take part in this conversation, and sat quietly, occasionally glancing at the silent old lady at the head of the table.

After the meal she rose and excused herself.

'I take it Dr Steele is calling to see my grandsons tomorrow, Miss Abbott?' asked Mrs Carrick. 'I shall want to see him before he leaves.'

'Very well, Mrs Carrick. Goodnight. Goodnight, Mr Fergus . . . Miss Grange.'

Fergus smiled as he rose, and held the door open for her. Celia ignored her completely.

The following morning, Lucy looked closely at little Ian, who was fretful, and decided to keep him in his cot. She sponged him down, noticing the rash on his chest, and put him into a cool, clean sleeping-suit. David seemed much better, so she dressed him in pale blue pants and a crisp white shirt, strapping his small fat feet into sturdy white sandals.

She was looking at Ian with concern when young Dr Steele arrived, and Lucy turned to smile at him with relief.

'I think Ian's got a heavier dose than David,' she said worriedly, and stood back while he examined the child, then wrote a prescription.

'Don't worry, Miss Abbott,' he said gently. 'He'll be all right.'

She smiled with relief, showing two delightful dimples, and Martin Steele found himself staring closely into her small pixie-like face, whose vivid blue eyes were regarding him steadily.

'I . . . I feel so responsible,' she said hesitantly.

'I don't suppose you carry German measles around ready to hand out to people,' he grinned cheerfully. 'Tomorrow they'll both be lots better and soon you'll have forgotten all about it. Young children catch their ailments very easily, you know.'

'I know,' she said gratefully. 'Goodness knows I've seen plenty of it in the past, but it's different when . . . when it's one's own . . . I mean . . .'

She broke off, biting her lip. How easy it was to give herself away! If she'd

58

said such a thing to Fergus, it could easily have aroused his suspicion. Worry clouded her eyes, and Martin reached out and squeezed her hand.

'You take things too seriously,' he said, squeezing her fingers. 'You need to get out a little more. Don't you have a day off?'

'Wednesday . . . today, in fact,' she told him, 'though I've put it off till next week.' She remembered that she was going over to see Nanny, though she planned to go by herself. Nessie was going to look after the boys until they were completely free of infection. 'I . . . I'll be going out.'

'I see,' he said, and she hesitated, wondering how to tell him that she was only going to see Nanny without appearing to hint that she would welcome an invitation out. Then his eyes twinkled teasingly.

'Is there a queue then for dates?' he asked. 'What about the week after? There's a concert on at the Town Hall, and I've got two tickets. We could have dinner first, then go straight to the concert.'

'I'd like that,' said Lucy shyly, and Martin Steele felt like dropping a kiss on her curly head, then remembered that he was a busy and ambitious G.P. and one of his best private patients was waiting for a word with him downstairs.

'Mrs Carrick is waiting for me,' he said briskly. 'Until the twentieth, then . . . Miss Abbott.'

'It's Lucy,' called David, who was beginning to take an interest in their conversation.

'Very well . . . Lucy,' laughed Martin. 'In a day or two young Ian will be as frisky as this young fellow.'

He rumpled the child's hair, and Lucy saw him out, then leaned back against the door. How nice he was, she thought. He was gay and good-natured, different from the unpredictable Fergus. If Stuart were anything like him, then she could understand Angela finding her marriage difficult. Poor Angela . . . being persuaded to elope, then having to pay for it ever since. If only she'd have better news of both her and Stuart soon!

There had been no letters to Nanny's, although she had written saying that the boys were being looked after without explaining the circumstances. Later she would tell Angela all about it, and hoped that her sister thought she'd done the right thing.

But at least Angela and Stuart couldn't be any worse, or the Carricks would be informed. As the day progressed, however, Lucy felt rather depressed, and as though in answer to her thoughts, Nessie came along to help prepare the nursery tea, and leaned over Ian's cot, putting a large cool hand on the little boy's hot forehead.

'You raise him up, Nessie,' said Lucy, 'while I give him this medicine.' Her voice was more coolly competent than she felt.

'Poor wee laddie,' sympathized Nessie. 'Mr Stuart's family has sure run into hard times. It fair makes ye think, wi' him runnin' away, though you'd think a' that would be in the past, and a' the bad luck ower noo. But there he is stuck in hospital, and his wife, and now the poor wee bairn's no' weel.'

'Then he's . . . he's still in hospital?' asked Lucy, her voice husky with anxiety.

'Oh, aye. Mr Fergus phones to Canada every other day. They're still just the same.'

Still just the same. Lucy repeated this to herself, and felt her throat go tight. She mustn't think too much about Angela, lying so many miles away. She must concentrate on doing her best for Angela's sons.

Her eyes were still dark when the door opened and Mrs Carrick came in on Fergus's arm, and came over to the cot without a word.

The small boy had been tossing restlessly, but his medicine seemed, at last, to be taking effect, and although his cheeks were still hot, he was beginning to sleep peacefully. Lucy forgot she was Miss Abbott, nursemaid, as she carefully smoothed the blankets and made the little boy comfortable.

The threatened tears now spilled over with relief, and she dashed them away impatiently, aware that Fergus and Mrs Carrick were regarding her with a hint of surprise. Suddenly the old lady pressed her small hand.

'It's all right, my dear. The baby is doing fine. You've done very well. You . . . you're a good girl.'

Lucy felt a strange softening in her heart as she looked at both of them, then she gave herself a hard mental shake. Whatever was she thinking about, feeling so drawn towards these two people who had helped to make her sister's life a misery for six years. Her features grew cool and composed.

'Thank you,' she said distantly.

The gentleness left the old woman's face, and she turned to her son with her customary imperious manner.

'We will go down to dinner, Fergus,' she said quietly. 'I take it you wish to have your meal here in the nursery, Miss Abbott?'

'Yes, please,' said Lucy.

The old lady nodded and turned away, and Lucy caught Fergus's cold eyes on her, a hint of anger in them. She was aware of having rebuffed both of them, and when the door closed, another tear slid down her cheek, this time unchecked.

3

Nanny was delighted to see Lucy again, hugging her warmly as she walked in the door, then examining her critically as if to reassure herself that she had not been eaten alive by the Carricks.

'Where are the bairns?' she asked, a note of disappointment in her voice.

'They've had German measles,' said Lucy ruefully. 'Sorry, Nanny, I'll just have to bring them next week, though I'll have to leave early. I have a date.'

'Who with?' asked Nanny suspiciously, and Lucy's dimples showed.

'Young Dr Steele,' she said, her eyes dancing. 'Any objections, Nanny?'

The old woman's eyes crinkled.

'Och no. It's time you enjoyed yourself, my lamb. Though . . . Dr Steele . . . hm.' She pondered, obviously turning him over in her mind. 'He seems a nice enough lad, very ambitious, I'd say. His dad used to have a butcher's shop on River Street and he was never over-generous with his measures. Always fair, but never over-generous. His mother was a Strachan and a quiet wee soul. I used to wonder if Adam Steele wasn't a hard man in the house.'

Lucy was laughing merrily.

'Oh, Nanny darling, how well you know everybody,' she said happily. 'When I do want to get married, I think you'd better arrange the match.'

'You'll be getting your bottom skelped again,' said Nanny darkly, though there was a twinkle of fun in her eyes. 'You could do worse, though, than one young man I can think of, but maybe you wouldn't agree with me. Haven't the Carricks tumbled to who you are yet?'

Lucy's face sobered as she shook her head.

'They mustn't, until Angela is better,' she said emphatically. 'They'd never give me the children, and I couldn't bear to have anyone else look after them now. Oh, Nanny, they are darlings. You'll love them.'

'Nae doot,' agreed Nanny.

'Are there still no letters from Angela?' asked Lucy, looking round. 'Nessie Cree says that Fergus phones Canada regularly and they're still just the same.'

'You would think Angela would have got one of the nurses to drop us a wee line, then,' grumbled Nanny. 'After all, she wrote to you before.'

'I know. I feel so worried at times in case she's worse.'

'She won't be any worse, lovey, or you would have heard,' comforted Nanny. 'Och no, she'll just not be bothering now you're sorting things out for her here.'

Lucy bit her lip. Angela was the only cause for disagreement between her and Nanny. The old woman had always felt that she ran out on Lucy, just when she needed her most. She didn't make allowances for the fact that Angela was only young at the time, and must have loved Stuart very much. Love could easily make girls behave foolishly, she decided, and thought of Martin Steele's warm brown eyes gazing at her admiringly. Then the dark arrogant features of Fergus Carrick began to intrude, and she gave herself a mental shake. It was the twins who needed her every thought and care at the moment. She was still very young, and had no wish to fall in love. It could only cause complications, and her life seemed to have become complicated enough already.

★ ★ ★

The following Wednesday, Lucy again took great care and thought over her choice of dress for her date with Martin. He had called several times to see the children, and had alternated between the brisk, professional young doctor and the friendly admirer. Lucy had looked forward to his visits, feeling very much in need of his friendship.

It had been an unpleasant week, mainly because she had been unwise enough to try to listen to a telephone conversation Fergus was making, when she realized he was asking for the hospital in Canada. Lucy's anxiety had got the better of her, and she had delayed her errand downstairs, hanging around the hall and hoping to pick up some news. She had listened openly when Fergus finally got through to the hospital, her heart beating furiously. Then it had nearly stopped with fright when she turned to find Mrs Carrick regarding her coldly.

'Miss Abbott,' she said, her voice like icicles, 'how dare you listen to my son's telephone conversation. If you were holding a permanent post in my household, you would be dismissed immediately. As it is, I'm strongly tempted to ask you to leave this house.'

Lucy was white and shaken. She knew she was completely in the wrong and cringed at being caught in such a humiliating position.

'I . . . I'm s . . . sorry,' she stammered.

'If my grandsons hadn't come to depend on you, you would go immediately,' said the old lady again, and Lucy turned away to hide the rush of tears to her eyes.

'Why did you do it?' Mrs Carrick asked, a faint softening in her voice.

Lucy bit her lip, then decided to tell part of the truth.

'I . . . I heard Mr Fergus asking for a Canadian number,' she said hesitantly. 'I wondered about the children's parents . . . how they were keeping . . . '

Fergus came out of the study, looking from one to the other, the haughty disdainful elderly woman and the wilting girl. He looked questioningly at his mother.

'How are they?' she asked. 'No, stay, Miss Abbott. You might as well hear, too.'

'Improving,' said Fergus briefly. 'Stuart will have the plaster off his leg next week, and Angela . . . ' he paused and glanced at Lucy . . . 'Angela also has a leg injury, but is making good progress.'

Lucy turned away with a muttered thanks. She hoped her obvious upset would be put down to being caught eavesdropping, and she felt ashamed of the whole episode. She'd always felt she could hold up her head in this household, but this had put her at a disadvantage.

The thought of her date with Martin had cheered her up, however, and now she went through her dresses, trying to decide on which one was most suitable and attractive. The days were now growing warmer while the trees grew lush and heavy with leaves, and the young green grass painted the fields bright emerald green in the rich sunshine. But the evenings grew very chilly and there was even a hint of frost now and again. Lucy was reminded of how she was 'ne'er to cast a cloot till May was oot,' according to Nanny.

So she lifted down a beautiful dress in rose velvet, trimmed with creamy lace, out of which her small head of soft black feathery curls rose like a flower. Her eyes sparkled like brilliant sapphires with excitement, as she enhanced them skilfully with eye shadow and applied a lipstick which reflected the colour of the dress.

A creamy cobwebby wool stole would be enough, she decided, as she picked up her evening bag, and walked downstairs to wait for Martin. Fergus came out of the lounge and stopped, staring, at the sight of her.

'Someone's in luck,' he told her, his black eyes snapping as he looked at her admiringly.

'Dr Steele,' she said quietly, and he nodded, pursing his lips thoughtfully.

'Nice enough chap,' he said quietly. 'Is . . . is it growing serious, Lucy?'

She felt her heart flutter a little at his use of her Christian name. He made it sound like a caress.

'We . . . we're just friends,' she told

him breathlessly, and again he nodded, as though deep in thought.

'Have a nice time, then, my dear,' he told her gently, and looked at his watch. 'Ah well, time I was moving. Mustn't keep Celia waiting.'

Lucy smiled and felt a strange sensation sweep over her . . . a sort of chagrined feeling which puzzled her. Why, she couldn't be jealous, could she? No wonder women were considered unpredictable creatures, she decided impatiently, when their own moods and emotions were incomprehensible to them. She didn't like the thought of Fergus dancing attendance on Celia Grange, yet why should it matter to her? She had no liking for Celia . . . but she mustn't lose sight of the fact that Fergus was a Carrick, and one of the people responsible for keeping her sister banished in Canada. If they'd had a spark of forgiveness in their natures, then they'd have asked Stuart to bring his bride back home again, and accepted her into the family.

Then this accident might never have happened, and Angela's life might have been a great deal easier. After all, Stuart had been an active partner in the business and could no doubt still be of value to the firm. Whenever she felt like softening towards the Carricks, she remembered these points. It was easy to get things out of perspective under their roof.

Martin arrived just as Fergus was leaving, and looked rather young and embarrassed as he walked in. Lucy gave him a dazzling smile of welcome, however, and his cheeks coloured as he stared at her with admiration.

'I'm glad we've got seats in one of the boxes,' he told her. 'Now that I see how lovely you look. I want to show you off to everyone.'

Lucy's eyes sparkled with delight.

'I've been looking forward to this all week,' she confided.

'Then let's get going,' said Martin, as he helped to wrap the stole round her shoulders. 'I've ordered a meal for us at the Copper Kettle. O.K.?'

It wasn't the smartest place, but it was small and cosy.

'O.K.,' said Lucy, and said goodnight to Nessie Cree, who admired her dress and sighed after them both romantically.

It was only when Lucy was settled in her seat at the concert that she realized how many people were present, and that she'd heard once already about this concert. Celia had been telling Fergus she'd got the tickets, and that 'everybody' would be there.

She and Fergus were certainly there, decided Lucy, rather uncomfortably, when she looked across from her excellent seat, and saw them in the opposite box. Fergus grinned wickedly, and made her a small bow, but she could see the cold fury on Celia's face. Again the other girl was elaborately dressed, her auburn hair upswept, and her neck and wrists sparkling with diamonds. Simon Grange, Celia's father, was the senior partner in a firm of solicitors, and the Granges had also owned property in Newton Stephens for several generations. Lucy knew them to be wealthy people, and was rather surprised that Celia even bothered to be angry when she saw her. Then she decided that no doubt the sight of an employee occupying a seat in the theatre every bit as good as her own offended her sense of propriety every bit as much as sharing the same dinner table.

Then Martin leaned forward to speak to her, and she relaxed and prepared to enjoy herself.

It was a delightful concert, the famous visiting orchestra in good form, and very much appreciated. Lucy almost managed to forget the other two in the opposite box, but not altogether. Again and again her eyes were drawn to Fergus, who appeared to be gazing straight at her. And once she caught the look of fury on Celia Grange's face, and it made her shiver with apprehension. She tried to pull herself together sensibly, telling herself that Celia had nothing to do with her, and couldn't possibly do her any harm. But there was a strange foreboding deep inside her, and she still felt cold and shivery, as though a goose walked over her grave.

In the car going home, however, Martin soon melted the ice.

'I mustn't be late,' she told him breathlessly, after they had sat talking in the car, 'in case I wake anyone going in.'

'All right,' he agreed quietly, and drove her out to High Crest.

'You will come out with me again, won't you, Lucy?' he asked gently, as she thanked him for the evening.

'Of course I will,' she assured him, and he slid his arms round her and kissed her gently.

'You're the loveliest girl I've ever known,' he said huskily, and wrapped her creamy stole round her, as though she were very delicate and precious.

'Goodnight, Martin,' she whispered,

feeling warmed and cherished. 'See you soon.'

The feeling lasted until she let herself into the house as quietly as she could, and started with shock to see Fergus standing in the hall. He must have been quick in taking Celia home, she decided, even if she lived close by.

'Well?' asked Fergus. 'Did you enjoy it?'

'Very much,' said Lucy primly, her small pixie face looking very pale in the dimmed night lights.

'Martin bring you home? He took his time,' said Fergus, advancing towards her, so that she could see his black eyes glittering strangely. She caught sight of the time and gasped a little, realizing that she and Martin had taken longer than she'd realized.

'We ... we were talking,' she defended herself.

'Perhaps he's a bit slow in getting round to things,' said Fergus. 'Is he, Lucy? Martin likes to calculate, you know.'

A moment later she was caught in his arms, and his mouth was down on hers, almost bruising her. She struggled wildly, like a small fluttering bird, but his arms were like steel bands round her slender body.

'I have less patience, Lucy,' he said, very softly, and she found she was sobbing with rage.

'You brute,' she whispered. 'I always knew I . . . I should h . . . hate you!'

'What a pity,' he drawled, 'when I don't hate you . . . not in the very least. Goodnight, Lucy.'

She stumbled up to her room, the tears of rage still on her cheeks. She should have been tired, but she felt more alive than she'd ever done in her life.

That night it was a very long time before she fell asleep.

★   ★   ★

Lucy expected an apology next day, but she didn't get it. To her relief, Fergus went off to Edinburgh on business, and Nessie informed her that he'd likely be away the best part of a fortnight.

'Does he often go away on business?' asked Lucy, casually.

'Noo and again,' was the reply. 'It used to be Mr Stuart was the one for gallivantin', and I think Mr Fergus only goes when he has to.'

Lucy digested this in silence, but she had little time to think of Fergus. Ian and David had now quite recovered from their attack of German measles, and had lost all their early shyness of their new and strange surroundings. Lucy now had her hands full keeping tabs on the pair of them, and decided that the best way to work off their energy was by taking them out in the fresh air.

They were still too young even for first steps in education, but she called in one day at a very charming toy shop in River Street, and bought one or two educational toys, which she hoped would keep them busy and their inquisitive minds entertained.

She managed to fit in several visits to Nanny Campbell, and the old woman was charmed with the little boys. They quickly responded to her open love for them, and were soon demanding visits to Nanny in the bus, when Lucy had neither the time nor the energy to take them.

Their nightly visits to Grandmother Carrick were also another event, and Lucy surprised herself by beginning to enjoy these as much as the other three. The old lady seemed to take on a different identity when the children burst open the door of the small study each evening, and clamoured for her love and attention.

Lucy often forgot to be on her guard, and chattered away like one of the family, joining in the general excitement when simple games were invented and thoroughly enjoyed.

Her days, too, were highlighted when Martin Steele sought her out, and took her out for the evening, or invited her and the children to accompany him for an afternoon drive. Their friendship developed like a lovely tender plant which Martin seemed to guard gently, as though fearful that it would break. Lucy knew that Fergus would consider it a milk and water affair, and sometimes, treacherously, she wished Martin would not be quite so slow. Then she'd blush at these thoughts, remembering Fergus's conduct on the night of the concert. Surely she could never approve of behaviour like that!

Then, suddenly, the warm balmy weather took a turn for the worse, and the skies blackened ominously. For a full day Lucy watched the rain pour down, rain such as one rarely saw in London, rain which filled the lochs and rivers and encouraged the countryside to grow lush and green.

The boys grew fretful in the nursery, quarrelling over toys and screaming at each other till Lucy's head ached.

That evening, even their grand-mother felt fatigued by them, and Lucy was thankful to see them both into bed.

'Aye, they've a lot o' Mr Stuart in them,' said Nessie sagely. 'Mr Fergus, too. Oh, he was a young ruffian of a boy, believe me.'

Lucy believed her, and surprised herself by realizing how much she missed him. Next day it still rained, but Lucy decided she'd had enough. If the twins got soaked to the skin, they were going out in it.

Swiftly she dressed them in their scarlet macs, sou'westers and matching gumboots, and ignored Nessie's head-shakings.

'I'll give them a bath when we get back, Nessie,' she said, 'but they badly need some fresh air, and I need to blow off steam. Poor Angela, I feel sorry for her sometimes.'

'Angela?'

Nessie Cree looked rather blank, then her eyes widened with surprise.

'I mean . . . Mrs Stuart,' said Lucy hastily, her cheeks scarlet. How easy it was to slip up! How lucky she had been up till now.

'Come on, you two,' she said hurriedly. 'Best foot forward, and no splashing through too many puddles!'

The twins loved it. They screamed with laughter, and raced along the wet streets, the water streaming down their faces. Lucy felt her curls clinging to her face in wet tendrils, and her boots beginning to squelch with water. She allowed the children to play as long as she could while they delighted in the water which squeezed out of their small red boots.

'Come on,' she called. 'Home!'

At first they protested vigorously, but exasperation lent her added authority.

'Come on!' she cried. 'Both of you. We're going home!'

A car slid to a halt, the water spraying from its wheels.

'Get in,' called Fergus, 'all three of you. What in the world are you doing out in this?'

'F . . . Fergus!' she faltered.

'Yes, Fergus,' he repeated. 'Put those

two in the back, though it will take my car days to dry out.'

'They w . . . were even w . . . worse inside,' said Lucy, her teeth beginning to chatter. 'I'll give them a bath when we get h . . . home.'

'Yourself, too,' said Fergus sternly. 'You look like a drowned . . . ' he paused and grinned, ' . . . kitten.'

Lucy wiped away a raindrop which had slid down her nose.

'Have you forgiven me yet?' asked Fergus softly.

'What for?' she asked stiffly.

'You know very well what for. I'm not going to apologize, though. Why should I when we both enjoyed it?'

Anger sparked from Lucy's eyes.

'I hate you treating me like a kitchenmaid!' she cried.

'Ah, ah . . . temper, temper,' he said soothingly. 'And believe me, my dear, I did *not* treat you like a kitchenmaid.'

She was silent, seeing that they were approaching High Crest.

'Are you busy on Wednesday?' asked

Fergus suddenly.

'N . . . not specially,' she said, still shaken.

'Then I would like you to come with me and see round Carrick's. Would you like to do that?'

She hesitated, momentarily taken aback, but the bait he offered was too great. She loved the large old bookshop, and it would be a delight to go all over it, at her leisure, with Fergus.

'I'd like that,' she said shyly, and he gave her one of his rare smiles, and squeezed water out of a black curl.

'Bath for all three,' he said sternly. 'As of now.'

'Yes, sir,' she replied meekly, the dimples back in her cheeks. 'Come on, children. Upstairs with Aunt Lucy.'

'Aunt Lucy!' they chanted, and her heart nearly stopped beating with fright as she realized what she'd said.

Happily Fergus was taking no notice, busy as he was with removing his luggage from the car boot.

Martin looked rather annoyed when he found out that Lucy had a date for the following Wednesday. He was now one of a group of doctors who examined patients at a new clinic instead of holding evening surgery, thereby ensuring some time off.

'It's too late to change now,' he grumbled, 'and my sister at Kilmarnock wanted to meet you. I thought we could have driven over to see her, then have dinner out.'

'I'm sorry, Martin,' said Lucy penitently, 'truly I am. But when Fergus asked me to go, I couldn't very well refuse.'

Martin saw the logic of this, and nodded, then smiled ruefully. He couldn't quarrel with the Carricks who were among his more important patients.

'Very well, Lucy,' he said graciously. 'It's just that I hate sharing you now. You've become very important to me, my dear.'

Lucy's eyes were soft. Martin was gentle and kind, and very restful. It was good to know that if ever she found things trying, she could run to him for comfort.

'I'm glad,' she said softly. 'It's good to know I have someone I can depend on.'

He bent and kissed her cheek.

'Anyway, I needn't be jealous when it's Mr Carrick. I expect it will be some sort of business outing, when he wants to take you to Carrick's. Only don't go dating anyone else!'

For a moment Lucy felt annoyed. Did Martin think she was such a nonentity that she couldn't attract someone like Fergus Carrick? Then she coloured faintly at her own thoughts. She had no wish to attract Fergus, and anyway, Celia Grange would see to it that she was no competition.

'I don't suppose you need worry,' she told Martin, lightly. 'See you soon.'

'Very soon,' he assured her.

★　★　★

Again Lucy found herself choosing her clothes carefully for her visit to Carrick's, finally deciding on her best suit in a soft misty-blue wool with matching accessories. Once again she brushed her feathery curls close to her head, and wore a discreet dab of expensive perfume to give herself confidence. Fergus aroused such a mixture of strong emotions in her. She was afraid of him, yet longed to be with him at the same time. He made her feel alive, and colour was whipping her cheeks at the prospect of a whole day in his company.

Glancing at her watch, she ran lightly downstairs just as he walked into the hall.

'Ah, there you are, Lucy,' he said briskly. 'Just on time. Wait for me in the car, will you? I've got a phone call to make.'

Lucy nodded and walked down the broad front steps to the comfortable

Rover which Fergus had chosen. It was pleasant to sit in his car, breathing deeply the mixture of scents which so reminded her of Fergus — pipe tobacco, old Harris tweed jacket, good leather and spicy shaving lotion. She shouldn't enjoy it so much, thought Lucy. But she did. And the thought of the day ahead caused her heart to beat rapidly with excitement.

Fergus joined her shortly afterwards.

'Sorry about that,' he said briefly, and for a moment his dark eyes rested on her flushed cheeks, and Lucy saw them glitter brightly before he turned away.

'All set?' he asked.

'All set,' she told him huskily.

At Carrick's, however, she completely forgot to be nervous when she walked through the heavy swing doors.

It was a beautiful old shop, rich with old polished wood and shining brass, where customers could spend as much time as they wished choosing a new book. Solid chairs, intricately carved, were placed around discreetly for the advantage of old people and Lucy was surprised at the very wide variety of books which were available.

'This section is mainly devoted to the classics and biographies,' Fergus told her, 'but through here we have paperbacks and beyond that, children's books. Upstairs we keep our pictures, glassware and leather goods, and in the basement we have a small museum section with a number of first editions which are not for sale, as well as secondhand books which are.'

This section was of special interest to Lucy, when Fergus escorted her down the rather narrow stairs.

'This old book is valuable, though unfortunately not quite perfect,' said Fergus, handing her a rather tattered copy of a book entitled *Poems Chiefly in the Scottish Dialect*. 'It is one of the famous Kilmarnock edition of Burns' poems.'

'I see,' said Lucy, looking through it with fascination. She was unaware of Fergus regarding her with a small smile softening the grim lines of his mouth. Lucy didn't have to pretend interest in Carrick's. She was obviously loving every moment of it.

'This one is by John Galt, and over here we have S. R. Crockett who wrote fine stirring tales about Ayrshire and Galloway. I can lend you other copies if you're interested.'

'Oh, please,' said Lucy. 'I think it's all fascinating.'

She lingered a long time over the books, loving their fresh inky odour, then Fergus escorted her upstairs to the stationery department, and through a small alcove into the fancy goods department, the walls lined with pictures. Many were original oils, hopefully offered for sale by local artists, though there were also a few prints of the Old Masters.

Lucy studied them all admiringly, then caught her breath as she recognized one small picture. It was an exciting picture of water tumbling over rocks, painted from an unusual angle, so that the water almost poured from the picture. It reminded her so much of a place she'd known as a child, only minutes away from her old home, and she felt her throat swell a little at the sight of it.

'It . . . it reminds me of the waterfall near Stanshaw Bridge,' she said.

'It is the waterfall near Stanshaw Bridge,' Fergus told her with a smile, and she tore her eyes away. There was no sense in allowing Fergus to see how much it meant to her, or he might wonder why, and question her. She would be no match for him, she knew.

Instead she hurried towards the lovely leather goods in soft deerskin and the fine handbags in polished leather and lizard skin.

'Some of this is hand-made locally,' Fergus told her. 'I find it more popular with tourists than cheap souvenir trifles.'

'I'm sure they are,' agreed Lucy, going over to look at some fine Stuart crystal. 'Some souvenirs are atrocious.'

She sighed a little as she walked back downstairs. The time had flown, but she had enjoyed every minute of it, and the evening ahead now seemed like an anti-climax. As though sensing her thoughts, Fergus put his hand on her arm as he guided her towards the car.

'How about a trip to Ayr?' he asked suddenly. 'We could have a meal there, then we might even go to the theatre.'

'Oh, I'd love that,' said Lucy, her eyes shining.

'Good,' said Fergus, settling her into the car.

As they drove off, Lucy had the uncomfortable feeling that she was being stared at, and as she turned quickly, she had a momentary glimpse of Celia's haughty face. It was so fleeting, however, that she wondered if she had been imagining things. She thought about it carefully, then put it out of her mind as the soft Ayrshire scenery was spread out like a carpet before her.

The Ayrshire coastline shimmered

like a jewel in the afternoon sun, the distinctive outline of Arran silhouetted against a blue sky softly painted with long red and silver fingers.

'There's Ailsa Craig,' said Fergus, pointing to a black rock shaped like a bun, rearing out of the sea.

'I know,' nodded Lucy, then bit her lip. As a child she had known this coastline well, but again she didn't want to be questioned by Fergus, so she contented herself by admiring it all silently, if nostalgically. Again it brought back memories of Angela, and warned her to be on her guard against this strong man by her side. She was enjoying his companionship, but she must look on it as one looked on a beautiful rainbow, to be enjoyed while it lasted, but soon to be gone. Sooner or later he would know that she was Angela's sister, then Fergus Carrick would never again be part of her life. But she would treasure this day as one of the most precious in her memories.

That evening she had to force herself to remember all this. It had been a wonderful meal, and she had thoroughly enjoyed the theatre. It had seemed so right for her to be sitting beside Fergus in the car, as though she was always meant to be there, and she sighed deeply as they approached Newton Stephens.

Fergus heard the sigh, and turned towards her with a smile.

'Tired, little Lucy?' he asked, so tenderly that her throat ached as she nodded.

'I've enjoyed it all very much,' she said, primly and politely. 'Thank you for taking me.'

He laughed softly.

'We must do it again soon,' he said, 'very soon.'

As he stopped the car, he turned to her, and Lucy had the instinctive feeling that he was about to take her in his arms, and shrank away in her seat. She could see the laughter leave his face, and his black eyes begin to harden. Then a smile again twisted his mouth.

'You look like a rabbit caught in a trap,' he told her, with a hint of contempt. 'What do you think I'm going to do . . . eat you?'

She turned away, colouring furiously, and it was his turn to sigh deeply.

'You'd better get to bed if you're so tired,' he told her briskly. 'Goodnight, Lucy.'

'Goodnight,' she whispered, and ran up the stairs, stumbling a little.

Next morning she found the lovely picture, giftwrapped, placed just inside her bedroom door. There was no note with it.

Lucy was now finding the children very much easier to manage. They had settled easily into routine and her natural love for them was soon returned in full measure. Lucy, Grandmother and Uncle Fergus became the centre of their small world, though Lucy was careful to speak often about their own parents when she had them to herself.

She wanted to make sure they wouldn't forget about Angela and Stuart.

Mrs Carrick seemed very satisfied with her handling of the children and treated her very graciously. If she hadn't been Angela's mother-in-law, Lucy would have loved her very much, seeing a charming person under the rather hard exterior.

Fergus seemed to be very busy, making a number of trips to Edinburgh, and Lucy was glad to keep out of his way. She felt the power of his presence too much, and could neither think nor act sensibly when he was about. Quite often she was asked to join the family for dinner in the evening, though rarely for lunch. She was glad about that, as Celia Grange was often in at lunch-time, and no doubt meeting Fergus in the evenings. She ignored Lucy completely, as though she had decided that the younger girl was beneath her notice.

The following week Lucy was happy to accept Martin's invitation to go to tea with his sister in Kilmarnock. Molly

Lawson was the wife of a school-teacher, she herself having taught before her marriage. She was most interested in Lucy's care of the two children, and asked some rather uncomfortable questions. Quite often Lucy had been tempted to confide in Martin her real relationship to the twins, but natural caution had prevented this, and she told herself that it was unfair to burden him with a problem which belonged entirely to her.

Lucy saw Martin look at her curiously and coloured a little as she side-tracked one or two questions.

'Yes, my father was a doctor in Newton Stephens, Mrs Lawson. I don't remember too much about his work, being rather young when he died, but I remember him telling me about my grandfather who had to work long hours in his surgery making up prescriptions. The practice was his before Father took it over, you see. I wonder what Grandfather Abbott would have thought of the Health

Service and places like the new Clinic where Martin sees his patients.'

'No doubt he had a large number of private patients, though,' said Martin. 'I have a large number of patients who are treated under the Health Service, but I must keep my private patients, too. They are very important, if I wish to build up a successful practice. No wonder most of our young doctors go off to America, you know.'

'I think a lot would depend on what you wanted to do with your money,' said Lucy.

'Not altogether,' disagreed Martin. 'We're lucky to have our new Clinic in Newton Stephens, but in some places it's rather heartbreaking with anti-quated buildings and equipment . . . '

This brought a general discussion, and Lucy felt rather relieved. She didn't know whether she liked Martin's sister or not, feeling that there was something a trifle self-righteous about her, and that she'd be very critical of Martin's friends. She was glad when they were again in the car, heading for Newton Stephens.

'It was kind of your sister to invite me,' said Lucy, more warmly than she felt. 'I must write and thank her, Martin.'

'Nice of you,' he said briefly, and for the next mile or two they drove in silence, then Martin cleared his throat.

'Lucy, I remember that you once asked me to keep the fact that Dr Abbott was your father confidential. Of course I wouldn't dream of betraying a confidence, but now that we're such . . . er . . . friends, I wonder if you'd care to tell me why.'

Lucy didn't reply immediately, then she sighed deeply. Of course Martin would have to know. He was gradually becoming important to her, and it was right that she should confide in him.

'My sister Angela is married to Stuart Carrick,' she said finally, after explaining all the circumstances. 'Ian and David are my nephews.'

'Your nephews!' echoed Martin, and

guided the car into a lay-by, turning to stare at her. 'Then the Carricks are related to you?'

She shook her head.

'Not to me. They're my sister's in-laws. Were you in Newton Stephens when she ran off with Stuart? I was only twelve then, but I believe it caused a stir at the time.'

Martin was frowning.

'I must have been away at school,' he decided, 'but Lucy, why didn't you tell me all this before, and why don't the children call you Aunt? Even the Carricks treat you like a Nanny . . . '

'They don't know,' she interrupted. 'That's why I wanted you to keep it all confidential.'

'But . . . '

'I'll try to explain,' she said hurriedly, and even as she started her long, rather garbled story, she knew she was making a poor job of it. Martin was looking at her incredulously, then sceptically.

'But won't they be annoyed when they find out?' he asked presently.

'Livid,' she assured him, and he turned away from her, frowning.

'I don't like it, Lucy. It's . . . it's deceitful.'

'I know,' she agreed, in a small voice, 'but it's allowing me to be near the children, and to look after them. Surely you can see that.'

'And surely you can see that you'll be rumbled sooner or later. Wouldn't it be more sensible to tell them . . . own up?'

Lucy bit her lip and began to wish she'd held her tongue. Then she shrugged. It was no use balming Martin for not seeing her point of view. He was so honest and straightforward that any hint of deception must be anathema to him. Now his eyes were full of concern, and she knew he must be worried for her.

'Perhaps,' she agreed, 'but the latest news of Angela and Stuart is better. Perhaps . . . perhaps all this will soon be over. I'll be able to own up just as soon as they can take the children again. But I won't hand them into any other woman's care until their mother is able to look after them again.'

Martin looked at the small chin, youthfully rounded, and was surprised by the strength and determination he saw there. There was a look of respect and admiration in his eyes as he slipped an arm round her.

'Be careful, my dear, won't you?' he asked, gently. 'The Carricks are influential people, and wouldn't like to be made to look like fools. It seems a pity you . . . er . . . aren't more acceptable to them and that the best of people often behave foolishly inside their own family circle.'

Lucy nodded agreement, though privately she wondered why it should matter so much to Martin. She was beginning to feel rather tired and depressed, and now that Martin had forced her to look at her present position, and on into the future, it seemed rather empty and frightening. She had behaved foolishly by using all these false pretences. It was no use pretending otherwise.

Now she turned to Martin with a small sigh.

'Well, it can't be helped now, can it? I mean, if they find out, they can't eat me, can they?'

4

The following evening Lucy was again asked to join the family for dinner, and was surprised to find Celia Grange already installed when she walked into the lounge, and even more surprised to receive a cordial smile.

'Ah, Miss Abbott!' she said, rather less condescending than usual. 'I haven't seen you for a few weeks. Are the children well?'

'Very well.'

'Dear little boys,' said Celia sweetly. 'A credit to you, I'm sure.'

Lucy blinked, then saw that old Mrs Carrick was nodding and smiling her approval. Perhaps Celia was trying new tactics, and had decided to show herself off as having a sweet nature.

Lucy's lashes dropped over her eyes. At any rate, Celia couldn't have seen her drive off with Fergus that day they went to Ayr, or she wouldn't be treating her in this friendly fashion.

A moment later Fergus arrived to join them, pouring himself a drink after seeing that the ladies already had theirs. He looked tired and a trifle abstracted, thought Lucy, and found herself studying him thoughtfully. She was often afraid of him, but as he sat down rather wearily, she felt her heart drawn to him with a queer nostalgic emotion. Suddenly she knew that every line of his face, the way a lock of dark hair fell over his forehead, and his habit of stooping slightly while in deep thought, were very dear to her. She loved every part of him, and even as she admitted it to herself, she dropped her eyes until she could collect her scattering thoughts. She loved Fergus, and felt as though everyone in the room must know, and must see this strong emotion sweeping through her. She would like to have excused herself and hidden herself in her room, but Mrs Carrick was already rising to lead the way into the dining-room, and asking for Lucy's arm.

Lucy wondered what the old lady would say if she could see into her heart, and if she would be ordered to leave the house immediately. She knew that the love was all on her side, however, and no doubt Mrs Carrick would give her silent sympathy, but would advise her to make a change just as soon as ever she could.

Lucy began to think of Angela with longing. At one time her own life had seemed so uncomplicated. It was Angela's letters which were so full of worries and troubles, and which had often depressed her after their arrival. But now it was her life which seemed to become more complicated every day. Fergus would never be for her. Apart from her relationship to Angela, Celia Grange would see to that. She had been practically jilted by Stuart for Angela, and it was inconceivable that Fergus would overlook her for Angela's sister!

This new strong surging emotion

could never bring her anything but misery, and Lucy had a sudden longing for London again, and was surprised by how much she loved the place. It offered peace and sanctuary, which were both very attractive at the moment.

She came out of her thoughts, startled, to find that Mrs Carrick had asked a question.

'I . . . I beg your pardon?' she stammered.

'I only require the salt, my dear,' Mrs Carrick said mildly, while Celia's laughter tinkled.

'It must be love, Miss Abbott,' she said slyly, while Lucy coloured vividly. 'Dr Steele, perhaps?'

Lucy was aware of Fergus surveying her flushed cheeks coolly and impersonally. He doesn't care, she thought miserably. He doesn't care whether I love someone else or not. I'm nothing to him.

'I'm sure Lucy's private life is no concern of ours, Celia,' Mrs Carrick pointed out with a touch of asperity, and Lucy smiled at her gratefully.

'Oh, isn't it?' asked Celia softly. 'Isn't it? I should have thought it would hold the greatest interest for you, Aunt Caroline.'

For a moment there was silence. Mrs Carrick and Fergus looked rather mystified, as did Lucy. The girl seemed to have old-fashioned ideas on domestic servants, and insisted on treating Lucy like one. But surely, to suggest that her free time should also be supervised was going a bit far.

'What are you talking about, Celia?' asked Fergus impatiently. 'Why should Miss Abbott's private life concern us?'

'Well, isn't she some sort of relation, after all?'

Lucy's heart nearly stopped beating. She saw the older girl's eyes on her, and felt like a rabbit trapped by the hypnotic stare of a snake. Celia Grange knew! She knew, and she was going to tell. The moment had come, and Lucy had never felt less prepared for it.

'Relation?' repeated Mrs Carrick, sharply.

'Surely you knew,' drawled Celia. 'I can't imagine anyone so . . . honest . . . as Miss Abbott keeping it from you, though it surprises me that the children don't call her, 'Aunt Lucy' more openly, since she is, after all, Angela Abbott's sister.'

Lucy heard the hiss of Mrs Carrick's indrawn breath, and her black eyes turned to survey Lucy like glittering black diamonds. She didn't care to look at Fergus, knowing that his face would now be every bit as granite hard as his mother's.

But she wasn't prepared for Fergus's drawling answer.

'But of course we knew, Celia,' he said quietly. 'Surely you don't think we would take an unknown person on to look after the children without checking references? I did that myself, as a matter of fact.'

Celia began to look bewildered, and Lucy, sitting beside Mrs Carrick, knew that the old lady, at any rate, hadn't known her true identity. Fergus must be covering up, no doubt wishing to avoid a row in front of Celia.

'But . . . but why?' she was floundering.

'Private family reasons, Celia,' said Fergus, smiling gently. 'Now, if you're ready, my dear, I shall take you home. I've had a busy day today, and there's an even busier one ahead of me tomorrow. We could all do with an early night.'

'Oh, all right,' said Celia crossly. She looked annoyed and disappointed, no doubt feeling that her plans had misfired on her.

'I think it's too bad, though, welcoming that girl into your house, after what her sister did to me . . . to all of us. How dare she! I would think twice before trusting her, believe me.'

'Goodnight, Celia,' said Mrs Carrick quietly, though Lucy could see her knuckles showing white as she clutched the arms of her chair, and her heart sank to her shoes. How had Celia found out? she wondered. There were going to be stormy scenes ahead, and she wasn't looking forward to them at all. She tried to gather the remnants of her dignity and righteous indignation round her, concentrating on the slighting way Celia had talked of her sister, implying that the Abbotts were not to be trusted. How dare she, thought Lucy.

But she only felt cold and miserable and very frightened. If only Martin were here! He'd help her. Loving Fergus wasn't much use when he didn't care at all for her in return. It gave her neither strength nor comfort.

Mrs Carrick stood up, and turned to her as Celia and Fergus disappeared.

'Now, miss,' she said, in a carefully controlled voice, 'please come with me to the study where we shan't be disturbed. I think we have something to discuss.'

Mrs Carrick opened the study door, and motioned for Lucy to sit down, closing the door firmly behind them.

Lucy drew a deep breath, trying to calm the fast beating of her heart, and knowing that to show herself afraid would immediately put her at a disadvantage. Her chair felt uncomfortable, and she reached behind her, to bring out a small toy car, painted brilliant red, with smooth rubber wheels.

Lucy cradled it in her hands, while Mrs Carrick very deliberately drew the curtains, and the sight of the toy car steadied her. It was the children who mattered, and Angela's rightful place in this house. The Carricks had shown little consideration for her sister, and would probably try to give her the same cavalier treatment. But they wouldn't find her so easy to browbeat.

Lucy tried not to think about the heartbreak this was going to cause her, now that she nursed a secret love for Fergus. It would be hard to fight him, or even his mother, but she clutched the small toy car in her hand, and faced the old lady bravely, as she sat down in her usual chair.

'I take it Celia has spoken the truth, otherwise you'd have been quick to deny you are Angela's sister,' she began, her voice as quiet and cold as ice.

'I'm Angela's sister,' nodded Lucy, with composure and a hint of pride as she lifted her chin.

'Then would you mind explaining yourself? Why didn't you come here openly, instead of pretending to be a nursemaid? Why did you find it necessary to keep your relationship to the children a secret?'

Lucy drew a deep breath.

'I did *not* come here under false pretences . . . not at first,' she added hastily. 'I came to claim the children, so that I could look after them for Angela. Later, when you mistook me for a girl sent along by the Agency, I . . . I decided to allow you to think so, and arranged things with the Agency later. It . . . it seemed the best solution, as I would have had to get a job in . . . in order to keep the children.'

Mrs Carrick's long hard face looked as though it had been carved out of stone.

'And how, pray, did you propose keeping my grandchildren if you could not afford to do so? How could you look after them efficiently, if you needed a job as well?'

Lucy began to wilt a little.

'Nanny Campbell would have kept them,' she said defensively. 'She looked after Angela and me when . . . when Mummy died, and . . . and later when Daddy died, too.'

'I see.'

The old woman tapped thoughtfully on the desk.

'Now, would you tell me why you thought it necessary to take charge of them at all? Did you imagine that my son and I were *incapable* of arranging the well-being of my grandchildren? Is that what you thought?'

Lucy bit her lip miserably, the small toy car growing hot and sweaty in her palm, then she felt anger stirring inside her. The children had been well looked after here, but only because they had had her to look after them. She'd been able to put up with their tantrums and tears, and had controlled their high spirits so common among twins, but mainly because she was the children's aunt, and had a natural love for both of them. Would a girl from the Agency have done so much? If the children had needed to depend only on Mrs Carrick and Fergus, would they have been so happy? Both their grandmother and Nessie were getting on in years, and Fergus was a busy man with little time to spare at home.

'I had not met you, Mrs Carrick,' she said evenly, 'and could only judge my sister's in-laws by their treatment of her. Although I haven't seen her since I was twelve, she writes to me regularly, and I keep all her letters. I know very well about what happened when she fell in love with Stuart, and they had to run away together before they could be happy. It seems to me shameful that such a thing should happen, that you think so little of my sister that the young couple had to hide in another country to be happy, and that you still don't accept her, even though she is your daughter-in-law.'

She paused for breath, and the old lady stared at her, her black eyes glittering and flags of colour burning in her parchment cheeks.

'Obviously you know nothing about it, child,' she said, coldly.

'I know *all* about it,' cried Lucy, her own temper making her eyes flash with blue lights. 'I know what Angela's life has been like for the past six years . . .'

She stopped for a moment, aware that Fergus had slipped through the door.

'Yes?' he asked softly. 'Do go on, Lucy.'

'I will,' she said breathlessly. 'I have it all down in black and white. Your precious Stuart is inclined to be a weakling, and Angela has had to be the prop for both of them . . . and the children. Whatever he's earned, he's spent, and she's had to pinch and scrape to feed and clothe her family . . .'

'You know nothing about it,' repeated Mrs Carrick tonelessly.

'It's *you* who know nothing about it,' insisted Lucy. 'You and Fergus here . . . what can you know about being poor, about worrying over new shoes for the children, and trying to make clothes last longer? What do you know about worrying how to pay the rent, and buy nourishing foods the children need, and . . . and still try to keep smart yourself? How do you think Angela manages on what Stuart earned when he spent most of it on himself? And . . . and how do you think I managed?'

'You?' Mrs Carrick's eyebrows shot up. 'What did you have to do with it?'

Fergus put up a hand.

'Please, Mother, let her finish. Yes, Lucy, tell us what you had to do with it.'

'I had everything to do with it,' she

told him, her voice still cracking. 'Who do you think Angela turned to when things got unbearable? I was all she had. I was all they *both* had, since neither of you felt obliged to worry about Stuart. I didn't earn a big salary, but they were welcome to the little I could spare. No doubt it kept the children from running barefoot, and might have given them a decent meal now and again. Please don't misunderstand . . . I . . . I was glad to do it.' Her voice was husky now. 'I . . . I've more right to those children than you have,' she cried. 'You've never done anything for them . . . anything! When I leave . . . tomorrow . . . I take them with me.'

'There will be no question of leaving tomorrow,' said Fergus firmly. 'The children remain here. They are our responsibility.'

'You're rather late in realizing it,' retorted Lucy.

'I told you, you know nothing about it,' said Mrs Carrick loudly. 'I regret your . . . your sister seems to have misled you. There was no need for them to elope. That they went ... under disgrace ... was their own choice, but they have never been cut off from this family.'

'Disgrace?' cried Lucy. 'What disgrace? Oh, of course ... Celia Grange. But you know, there are two interpretations of being cut off from a family. They have their pride. Were you waiting for them to crawl to you?'

Mrs Carrick rose slowly to her feet.

'Obviously it is useless to talk to this young lady. You must excuse me, I wish to go to bed. We will make proper arrangements in the morning.'

She rose and Lucy watched her go, feeling suddenly drained. She had fought them both, but she could not feel victorious. Fergus had escorted his mother from the room, and now he returned and looked at her coolly.

'You're like a little cat with all its claws showing,' he told her.

'I have to be,' she said tiredly, 'to fight you.'

'Why fight? I knew all along you were Angela's sister.'

Her mouth flew open.

'You . . . you really *knew*!' she gasped. 'But how . . . ?'

'Easily,' he said, laughing a little. 'Your name . . . Abbott . . . it isn't really so common, you know. Then a word with the Agency, or had you forgotten that? I checked on you, and found you were Dr Abbott's youngest daughter. Then, of course, you gave yourself away several times. You're an awfully poor actress, you know.'

Lucy was almost speechless with mortification.

'And did your mother know, too?'

He shook his head, obviously enjoying her discomfiture.

'No, I didn't tell her.'

'Why not?'

'I . . . er . . . waited for her to get to know you a little better.'

Lucy digested this silently, but could find no sense in it.

'Why?' she asked, a note of genuine

curiosity in her voice, but Fergus only shrugged.

'So you've been laughing at me all the time,' she said sadly, 'even when you took me out ... that lovely day in Ayr ... '

He caught her fingers and squeezed them till they hurt.

'You're wrong, my dear,' he said quietly, 'as wrong as you are over Angela. We've done nothing to be ashamed of in that direction, nor am I ashamed of taking you to Ayr. It was a day to remember. Try to believe that.'

She pulled her hand away, trying to get used to the fact that he had known about her all along, and had pretended that he didn't. She felt as though her heart was bleeding.

'It's possible we may have different standards, Fergus,' she said, her face white. 'May I go to my room now after I've made a telephone call?'

His own face hardened.

'Very well,' he said coldly. 'You obviously refuse to accept my word that my family have done nothing at all to cause us any shame, and have behaved with propriety towards your sister. Obviously my word is not good enough for you.'

She said nothing, but brushed past him and walked on trembling legs to the telephone. She must ring up Martin. He would help her . . . advise her what to do. Somehow she must get the children away, though that was going to be difficult. Neither she nor the Carricks were going to be willing to give them up now.

But whatever they said, the facts spoke for themselves, she thought, remembering the poor shabby clothing the children had when they arrived. If the Carricks had helped them, wouldn't the children have been well-dressed?

Martin sounded tired after an evening on duty at the Clinic, but he brightened when Lucy spoke to him on the telephone, and was free to meet her for lunch the next day. Nessie could always manage to give the children a bit of attention after their early lunch. She loved helping out like that now and again.

'See you then, Martin,' said Lucy, and felt a bit better when she put down the receiver. This was short lived, however, when she turned to find Fergus at the bottom of the stairs.

'You won't be able to do much crying on Steele's shoulder,' he told her, his eyes gleaming. 'Don't be mistaken about that, Lucy.'

She flushed scarlet.

'How dare you listen to my telephone conversation!' she cried.

'Why not? You listened to mine!'

She almost cried with shame. 'How like you to remind me of that! Especially since you must have known why I did it.'

'I did,' he said coolly, 'and if I hadn't, you'd have been out on your pretty little ear. Look, Lucy, why can't you just carry on as before, only consider yourself one of the family? Don't go working out stupid ideas with Steele. He can't help you and I don't have to spell it out for you to understand why. He's . . . ambitious, you know.'

'Perhaps you're applying your own standards to Martin,' defended Lucy.

'Oh, I wouldn't,' protested Fergus. 'I doubt very much if Steele would ever have my standards. I wouldn't dream of applying them to him!'

'He's worth ten of you,' she said, as she brushed past him, and wished that she believed it. 'He's a gentleman.'

Fergus caught the skirt of her soft woollen dress and pulled her back into his arms.

'What a drawback . . . being a gentleman,' he said laughingly, and a moment later she was struggling wildly as he kissed her.

She lay in his arms like an exhausted bird, tears of shame on her eyelashes. Because whatever she ought to feel about Fergus bore no relation to what she did feel for him. She loved him, and hated herself for it.

'I wouldn't have done that if you hadn't enjoyed it too,' he told her.

'Let me go!' she cried, wrenching herself free, and ran upstairs to her room.

5

'You don't look too well slept, Miss Lucy.'

Nessie Cree looked at her solicitously next morning, as Lucy rose, heavy-eyed, to dress the children and give them breakfast. She nodded, unsmilingly, aware of Nessie's curious glances, then shrugged resignedly. Nessie lived in, and could hardly have failed to hear most of what went on the previous night. No one had troubled to keep their voices down, and Nessie was still busy clearing up from dinner.

'You heard, didn't you, Nessie?' she asked.

'I could hardly help it, Miss Lucy,' the older woman said, a twinkle of humour in her bright black-button eyes. 'I'm no deaf yet.'

Lucy busied herself wiping milk off Ian's chin.

'These two are my nephews,' she acknowledged. 'I'm Angela's sister.'

'Ye're no' like her, if I may say so, Miss Lucy,' commented Nessie dryly. 'Her bein' fair and you bein' dark, I mean,' she added hastily.

'Did you know her well?' asked Lucy. 'I was only twelve when she went away, you know, Nessie. I remember the rows, and hearing talk at school, though Nanny Campbell tried to keep most of it away from me.'

'Janet Campbell's a good sowl,' commented Nessie. 'A lot o' folk thought Miss Angela should have showed her more consideration, leavin' her wi' . . . Oh, well, never mind, Miss Lucy. It's all in the past. There's been enough inquests, and now the poor young things have had mair bad luck than they deserved.'

Lucy nodded and absently separated the small boys who were quarrelling over the empty cornflake packet. They were now better disciplined, but still far from easy to manage, and Lucy often felt that she had her work cut out to keep them out of mischief.

'I'm seeing Mrs Carrick at ten,' she told Nessie. 'Then I'll take the children out for a walk. I wonder, though, Nessie, if you or Rosie could just keep an eye on them after lunch while I slip out. There's . . . someone I want to see.'

'Of course, Miss Lucy. Er . . . will you be gone long?'

'Not long,' she was assured, and this time Nessie's natural curiosity had to remain unsatisfied.

Lucy's interview with Mrs Carrick was brief but painful. The old lady looked tired in spite of her inflexible manner, and Lucy felt a stab of regret that she'd been to blame.

'I . . . I'm sorry about this, Mrs Carrick,' she said apologetically, and the stern features wavered for an instant.

'I'm sure you are,' she said briskly, and Lucy flushed with annoyance.

'My son and I have decided to ask you to remain here with the children until their parents are well. They will fly from Canada just as soon as both are well enough to travel. The children's journey here was admirably arranged, in the care of the stewardess, but naturally they cannot go back the same way. In the meantime, there can be no question about you taking the children away, and as you seem to feel responsible for them, it's best that you remain here. Your salary, of course, will be amended since the relationship is not an ordinary one between nursemaid and children.'

Lucy coloured vividly.

'I was hoping to discuss that with you,' she said stiffly. 'Since I am related to the children, and feel they are my responsibility, I . . . I'd prefer not to accept any salary from you . . . '

'Don't be ridiculous, girl,' rapped out the old lady. 'You said yourself you would need to find a job.'

'I have a little money,' said Lucy proudly.

'Then may I suggest you take better

care of it than your sister would!'

The old lady's eyes were snapping with anger, and Lucy, in turn, felt that she wanted to run out of the house and never come back. How they disliked Angela! They would never forgive her for intruding into their precious family.

Lucy was glad she hadn't been asked for any promise to remain here with the children. If she were to listen to insults against her sister, then she would leave immediately for Nanny Campbell's and take the children with her. She thought of Martin and longed for lunch-time to come. He, at least, would help her, and the knowledge that she had a friend on whom she could count gave her an inner strength.

'I shall accept a salary . . . my present one,' she conceded. 'No more.'

'Very well,' said the old lady. 'The choice is yours.'

Yes, the choice was hers, thought Lucy, as she walked off to meet Martin. She thought of Fergus and her heart went cold. How long would she be able to stand this state of affairs? She would be unable to keep out of his way, as Mrs Carrick now insisted that she join the family for meals. She was, in fact, to be treated like the traditional poor relation, and the thought gave her no pleasure at all.

Martin smiled with pleasure when he saw her, in the small quiet restaurant where they'd arranged to meet.

'I'm not awfully hungry, Martin,' she told him, and he eyed her solicitously.

'Feeling all right, dear? You aren't over-doing things, are you?'

'Not really. It's just . . . Martin, the Carricks know. They know I . . . I'm Angela's sister.'

She heard his indrawn breath.

'Ah,' he said carefully. 'And how did they take it?'

She pursed her lips.

'A bit stormy in Mrs Carrick's case, but Fergus knew all the time.'

'Did he?' cried Martin. 'Why didn't he tax you with it, then?'

'He was waiting for me to tell them,'

said Lucy, rather bitterly.

'Then you haven't been asked to leave?'

She shook her head.

'No, they want me to stay, but . . . oh, Martin, how can I? I don't know how long I'll be able to stand it.'

Martin looked at her questioningly, and began to eat his soup, motioning for her to do the same. Lucy picked up her spoon, but the hot liquid almost stuck in her tight throat.

'I . . . I'm not very hungry,' she said.

'Eat it up,' he told her. 'We can't waste good food,' and she felt like one of his patients. 'You'll feel better afterwards. I can't see that anything has changed so much. In fact . . . '

'Oh, but it has!' broke in Lucy. 'Don't you see, when I was just the nursemaid, they never discussed Angela in my presence. Now I have to listen to insults about her. Mrs Carrick even insulted me by trying to offer me more money now she's found out I'm related to the children.'

Martin looked quizzical, as he began to attack his dinner.

'Not much of an insult, Lucy, to be offered more money.'

'I don't want to be paid to look after my nephews,' she said fiercely. 'I don't want to be beholden to the Carricks.'

'Very altruistic, but not very practical, my dear,' said Martin teasingly. 'How else could you manage?'

'I'd manage somehow. I hate being at High Crest under these conditions, though I certainly won't give up the children.'

'Of course not,' he agreed soothingly. 'Do eat up, Lucy.'

The food felt like sawdust in her mouth, and she looked at Martin's enjoyment of it with something like wonder. How calmly he took things! Nothing seemed to ruffle him at all.

'Martin,' she said urgently, 'would . . . would you help me?'

He smiled reassuringly.

'Of course I will, my dear.'

'Then . . . then if things get very bad,

and I . . . I want to take the children to Nanny's, could you take us there in your car? It would be too much for me to manage on the bus.'

The smile left his face.

'Good heavens, Lucy, don't be ridiculous, my dear. How could I possibly drive up to High Crest while you load the children and their luggage into the car? What do you think the Carricks will be doing? Waving you away?'

Lucy flushed and felt a stirring of anger. There had been a sneering note in Martin's voice.

'Of course I don't think that,' she said sharply. 'I . . . I would take them out for a walk as usual, and . . . and meet you somewhere. It's just that . . . if Fergus got suspicious, or even Mrs Carrick, they'd soon find me at the bus station. I might not have time to get away, but once I'm at Nanny's, then they mightn't find things so easy.'

Martin laughed indulgently.

'Darling Lucy,' he said gently, 'don't

136

you think you're dramatizing yourself a little? What could you gain by running away? Nothing at all. But think what you could gain by staying! The Carricks now think of you as a young relative, and you could be almost like a daughter in the house . . . if you are clever. They're influential people, and can be of great help to you . . . to both of us.'

'Both of us?' cried Lucy.

'Of course, darling.'

Martin took her hand.

'We may want to marry one day, and if we're to have a good life together, it would be madness for me to offend one of my best private patients. And if I encouraged you to go against their wishes, believe me, I would offend them. So you see how impossible it is!'

Lucy was staring at him, white-faced.

'I see,' she said quietly, and wondered why she hadn't seen long ago. Of course everything must take second place to his ambition with Martin. She ought to have seen long ago that he pandered to the Carricks. In fact, it was pleasing him that they now knew she was some sort of kin to them, and they hadn't turned her out. That was making her more attractive to him, and he was even mentioning marriage for the first time.

She felt hollow inside. She'd been so sure Martin cared for her, and that she could depend on him if ever she was troubled or unhappy. Now all that had turned to sawdust, and she closed her eyes, seeing Fergus grinning at her again.

'You won't be able to do much crying on Martin's shoulder,' he had said.

And how right he had been! Martin didn't want her crying on his shoulder. Instead he wanted her to insinuate herself with the Carricks, in order to further his career!

She felt her face go cold and expressionless, as Martin reached again for her hand.

'Why don't you just do as they ask?' he said softly. 'Stay on and take care of the children until your sister comes home. It's so sensible, dear. It really is. People like us can't afford pride, you know. We have to learn acceptance. You see that, don't you?'

She nodded.

'I see lots of things, Martin,' she said quietly.

'Good,' he smiled. 'And don't worry about the future. After this job is over, I may have another one waiting for you.'

He patted her hand as they left the restaurant.

'Can you get the bus back, Lucy? I'm afraid I've some appointments to keep now.'

'Of course,' she said tonelessly. 'Goodbye, Martin.'

'Au 'voir, surely,' he smiled. 'Cheer up, my dear. We must arrange a night out soon again. That'll cheer you up.'

She watched him go, then turned her steps towards the bus stop, hesitated, and decided to walk. Somehow she must clear her head a little, and take hold of herself again before going back to High Crest.

It was a warm sunny day, but she hardly noticed the laughing, hurrying crowds, or felt the warm pavements beneath her dainty white sandals. A car slid almost silently to a stop beside her.

'Lucy! *Lucy!*'

She started, and turned round half-fearfully.

'Get in,' said Fergus, and she obeyed without argument.

'Well?' he asked roughly. 'What did he say? I saw you both leave the Willow Tree.'

She didn't answer, but glanced at his profile. He looked sombre.

'What did Steele say, then?' asked Fergus again. 'Has he asked you to marry him, and offered a home to you and your nephews who are so precious to you? Has he offered you sanctuary in case we Carricks all turn nasty to you?'

Lucy fought to control a sudden lump in her throat.

'Just . . . leave me alone!'

'Delighted!' said Fergus, 'only understand this Lucy. Don't you dare leave

High Crest with my nephews. Any mad schemes you've thought up, you can forget. You've taken on a job and, by heaven, you finish it, so no running out. Is that understood?'

She nodded and wiped her face with a wisp of a handkerchief. She understood all right, but there was no reason why she should agree with all he said, was there?

6

After a few days, Lucy found that her life had settled down again into a routine the same, yet in many ways very different, as it was before. Mrs Carrick insisted that the children now call her 'Aunt Lucy', and that she mix with the family as much as possible. This was made easier by the fact that Fergus was quite often in Edinburgh.

She learned that Celia, too, had been in London, and was treated to a look of anger when she dropped in one day, and found Lucy being treated as one of the family.

'You still here, Miss Abbott?' she asked, pointedly.

'Lucy will remain here to look after the children while it is necessary,' said Mrs Carrick coldly.

Celia took the hint, and managed a frosty smile.

'Oh, good . . . very good . . . er . . . Lucy,' she said condescendingly.

Nanny Campbell, too, was relieved when she found out the Carricks knew the truth, and were still willing to accept her.

'I always thought they were no' sae bad,' she said, nodding wisely. 'They could have insisted on keepin' the bairns and asking you to leave, Miss Lucy, though I'd have been fair mad if they had.'

Lucy smiled.

'They could see I meant it when I said I would never give up the children,' she said evenly.

'Well, you should be happy noo,' commented Nanny, and cast a sideways glance at Lucy's pale face. There was something different about the girl, as though she'd been through some sort of experience which had saddened her, and drained her spirit.

'You're not, though, are you, lovey?' she asked, gently. 'Have you and Dr Martin quarrelled? Ye havena mentioned him for a while.'

Lucy shook her head slowly.

'Not quarrelled exactly, Nanny,' she said evasively.

She thought of Fergus, and how much he had come to mean to her. Just to catch a glimpse of him was enough to set her heart beating wildly, then settle down to a quiet yearning, when she remembered that her love for him would never come to anything.

She felt that she was being a fool, and had no wish to confide in Nanny. It would only upset the old woman. It was much better to let her think she was upset over a quarrel with Martin, so she forced a smile.

'Nothing very serious, Nanny, I promise you.'

'That's good, my lamb. I hate to see you unhappy.'

Lucy stared out of the window at the green fields behind Nanny's cottage.

'If . . . if anything ever happened, and . . . and I wanted to come back here,

Nanny . . . would you mind?' she asked hesitantly.

'What a question!' cried Nanny. 'If ye want to gie me the huff, just ask it again. This is your home, my love, any time you need it.'

The gentle voice soothed Lucy's sore heart.

'I knew it would be too much for you, Miss Lucy,' Nanny said quietly. 'It was too much responsibility for a bairn, because that's a' you are.'

'I feel a fool, Nanny,' sighed Lucy. 'I feel such a fool.'

Gradually, however, her depression lifted and she began to feel happier than she'd done for days. A few days later she found herself singing as she prepared to take the children for a walk.

Fergus watched her walking lightly downstairs, a small boy on each hand. They were looking brown and healthy, and their rosy faces shone brightly.

'You all sound very happy,' he commented.

'It's the weather,' Lucy told him.

'Isn't it a gorgeous day? We could do with a visit to the seaside.'

As soon as the words were out, she could have bitten them back. It sounded so much like an invitation.

Fergus was looking at his watch.

'Why not?' he asked lightly. 'I can afford some time off.'

'Please don't trouble,' she said hastily. 'I . . . er . . . I was thinking of other arrangements.'

The smile left his eyes.

'Steele no doubt,' he said coldly. 'But I'm quite capable of arranging an outing for my nephews, if I wish to take them. Unfortunately I must ask you to accompany us. I doubt if I could manage them on my own.'

'Very well,' she conceded quietly. 'If you'll allow me to collect a few things for the beach, and tell Nessie I can be ready in about ten minutes.'

'Good,' said Fergus. 'Would you prefer Girvan, or Ayr, or a quiet spot like Lendalfoot?'

She avoided his eyes.

'I'll leave that to you, Fergus,' she told him.

'Girvan then,' he said briefly. 'I've no doubt the boys can enjoy some ice cream and a trip out in a rowing boat. Girvan can supply both.'

She nodded, and a moment later he was gripping her shoulders.

'Perhaps we don't see eye to eye about some things, Lucy,' he said quietly, 'but I refuse to take a miserable lump of cold hard rock beside me in the car all the way to Girvan. Maybe you'd prefer Steele's charming company, but you'll have to make do with me, and by heaven, you're going to look as if you're enjoying yourself. So get that nice smile back on again and you can even start singing if you like. You weren't so miserable five minutes ago.'

Her blue eyes were wide as they met his, seeing the strength and determination in his face. She couldn't argue with him, she knew. She would only give herself away. A wavering smile touched her lips, and his own face softened into an answering smile.

'It's the children's day, Lucy,' he said softly. 'Just remember that, so let's all enjoy it, shall we?'

She nodded.

'All right, Fergus.'

The boys were delighted to go with Aunt Lucy in Uncle Fergus's car. As they drove out of the gates, the hood down and the wind whipping colour into Lucy's pale cheeks, she caught sight of Celia Grange making for High Crest.

'There's Miss Grange,' she remarked to Fergus, and he waved gaily. There was no answering smile or wave from Celia, though she stared after them.

'I wanted a word with Celia,' commented Fergus, almost to himself. 'I expect I'll see her tomorrow.'

It wasn't a specially good start to the day, but no one could remain depressed for long, as Fergus guided the car along fairly narrow but well-surfaced roads, tree-lined, with magnificent views of gentle hills and bright well-kept farms.

Often the road ran beside a broad tumbling river, startling a heron into flight.

Soon, however, they could see the long blue expanse of sea, with Ailsa Craig a stone's throw away, and the outline of Arran dimmed by mist.

'There's some big boats going to Ireland,' said Fergus, and the twins were quiet for once, their eyes on the ships which could be seen quite clearly. 'And there's a plane making for Prestwick. Your mummy and daddy will be coming on one quite soon.'

But again the boys were silent.

'I hope it won't be long before they're here,' commented Lucy, thinking it sad that the children might be forgetting their parents already.

'I agree,' said Fergus roughly, 'since you're so obviously determined to do your duty, and can't wait to leave High Crest. What's wrong, Lucy? Steele getting impatient?'

She wanted to tell him that Martin meant nothing to her now, but she didn't feel like arguing any more.

'Girvan,' she read, passing the signpost into the town. 'We're nearly at the seaside now, boys.'

The twins shouted excitedly, and suddenly Fergus and Lucy were laughing with them.

'It's the children's day,' Fergus had said, and Lucy bent all her energies in seeing that it was.

It was late afternoon when Fergus drove them all home again, while Lucy cuddled two sleepy little boys. It had been a wonderful day, and for a while she had pretended to herself that they were all part of her own family. Maybe it didn't help though, she thought sadly, to glimpse what life could be like, if only circumstances were different.

She sat quietly, dreaming her dreams, till they again reached Newton Stephens, and Fergus drove quickly up to the front door. How nice it would be if the day wasn't quite over, thought Lucy, and if only she could go dancing, or somewhere, with Fergus. But he, too, was quiet, as he helped her in with the children, and soon Lucy was busy giving them supper, and putting them to bed.

That evening she and Mrs Carrick dined alone. Fergus had gone out, no doubt to see Celia Grange, thought Lucy heavily. Lucky Celia . . .

A few days later Lucy was busy in the nursery with the children when she heard light footsteps approaching the door. It opened after a light tap, and Celia Grange stood there, smiling happily, two large parcels in her arms.

'Aunt Caroline said I could come right up, Lucy,' she said sweetly. 'I've brought a golliwog each for the children. Hello, darlings. Got a kiss for Aunt Celia?'

The small boys ran towards her a trifle hesitantly. Celia had never made much fuss over them in the past, but the removal of the paper bags from the bright golliwogs was enough to do the trick, and they rushed towards her, hugging her till her elaborately dressed hair was in danger of collapse.

'All right! All right,' she said sharply, and Lucy could see the irritation and impatience on her face. Clearly Celia's motive for visiting the nursery wasn't a growing love for the children. However, when she stood up, smiling brightly as she watched the small boys examining their new toys, her eyes had softened as she turned to Lucy.

'They really are darlings, aren't they?' she asked sweetly. 'No wonder you love them, Lucy. At first I could only remember that they belonged to Stuart, and . . . and might have been mine.'

Her voice wobbled a little, and Lucy blinked at this new Celia.

'But we must let bygones be bygones, mustn't we?' she asked, with a small smile. 'After all, they're Fergus's nephews, and of course, no woman can stand out long against a couple of beautiful children.'

'No, I suppose not,' said Lucy, finding her voice.

'Anyway, I came to see you, too, my

dear,' went on Celia, lowering herself into a wicker chair. 'Will you be free at any time today?'

Lucy frowned.

'Well, I could spare an hour in the afternoon when the children have their nap.'

'Good,' beamed Celia. 'I understand that you can type, my dear, and I have some papers to get ready for Daddy. He has an important meeting tomorrow and his typist is off sick. I *can* type a little, but I'm very slow and rather ragged.'

'Of course,' said Lucy, 'I'll be glad to help.'

'It's just a small report,' smiled Celia. 'We have property in this area, and I help out as factor, you see.'

'I see,' said Lucy.

She still felt rather bewildered. This was the first time Celia had ever gone out of her way, even to speak to her, let alone ask for her help, and she wondered what could be behind it. Was she at last recognizing that Lucy was part of the family, even if it was a very small part? Was she trying to say that she no longer regarded her as an outsider?

The girl was very beautiful and charming when she removed her haughty expression, thought Lucy, and remembered Fergus. She could well understand him falling in love with Celia Grange, because this was how he would see her. There would be no arrogance in her manner towards Fergus.

'Would you care for coffee?' she asked Celia. 'I usually have a cup at this time, while the twins have their orange juice.'

'No, thank you, my dear,' said Celia, rising and smiling sweetly. 'I must go now. Can you come at about two-thirty?'

'Yes, of course.'

'Good. I'll look out for you. Good-bye, children,' said Celia. Rising she side-stepped them neatly, and slipped through the door, closing it quietly.

Lucy watched her go, her forehead wrinkled in thought. It would certainly be more pleasant all round, if Celia decided to be friendly. She felt badly in need of a young person's friendship, now that she could no longer rely on Martin. She still saw him, very occasionally, and had made it clear that there could never be anything more than that between them. He had accepted that, but Lucy sometimes wondered if the message had gone home, or if he thought she was just in a mood. But even if she didn't love Fergus, she could never marry Martin. He was far from being her type of person.

Lucy drank her coffee, and went along to see Nessie about listening for the children, while she was out. She was a good typist, and would soon do Celia's report. It would be a pleasant change from mending small torn jeans.

Celia Grange's home wasn't quite so large as High Crest, but it was much

155

more luxuriously furnished and carpeted, the furniture of a new modern design. Celia's study could only be called that because of a small desk in the corner. It was much more like a small sitting-room, the colour scheme of soft greens and greys, with vivid splashes of colour in the orange and yellow cushions. Lucy looked round with appreciation. Perhaps Celia had gone to great lengths to study home decoration before planning her own home, but there was no doubt she'd managed it beautifully. It even managed to look lived-in.

'This is lovely,' she said sincerely, sitting down in the chair indicated. 'Did you choose it all, Celia?'

The older girl nodded complacently.

'I've managed this house since Mother died five years ago,' she said, going over to the desk. 'I don't think Father has had any reason to grumble. A woman must be an asset to a man, and see that his home is a suitable background for him. That's why it

156

seems to me such a . . . pity . . . when a man marries quite the wrong girl. It's a wasted life . . . or don't you agree?'

'Oh, of course,' said Lucy hastily, thinking of High Crest. She loved the old furniture there, and if her advice had ever been asked, she wouldn't have changed a single thing about it. She tried to imagine the old house after Celia had managed it for a few months, but couldn't picture these bright modern rooms against the background of quiet restrained elegance which was High Crest.

'Here's my report almost ready for Daddy,' said Celia, picking up a large folder. There was a sheaf of papers covered with small neat figures, and another folder to which had been clipped several typed pages.

'Miss Tempest did these for me,' Celia went on, leafing them over. 'There's only one left to do. Here it is.'

Lucy took it and walked over to the typewriter where Celia had laid out quarto paper and carbon.

'Two copies, please,' she said graciously, 'and I'll make some tea for when you've finished. It probably won't take too long.'

It wouldn't have taken Celia long either, thought Lucy, puzzled, even with two fingers. She fitted the paper into the typewriter, then picked up the written pages, catching her breath when she saw the heading.

'Report on Condition of Airlie Cottage, Glenbanks, should it become expedient to sell this property.'

Lucy felt a trifle light-headed as she stared at the address, and knew straight away why she had been asked to type the report. This was Nanny's cottage . . . and it was rented from Mr Grange! Somehow it had not occurred to Lucy to wonder if Nanny rented her cottage. She had always just assumed it was her own property, yet even as she typed the report, her face white and her lips compressed, she was remembering that the old lady had never been very well off. She had been rather presumptuous in thinking she owned the cottage.

Yet why had Celia really asked her to type this? Obviously it was a subtle way of telling her that they owned Nanny's cottage, and had the power to sell it if they wished.

Lucy caught her breath again, and her chin firmed. Celia must have something in mind, and somehow she must be ready for it. She wasn't going to allow the other girl to shake her composure like this. Carefully she typed the rest of the report, reading that the cottage was in an excellent state of repair, and it had been well maintained outside and in. She gasped a little when she saw the estimated value of the cottage. Truly, the value of property in and around Newton Stephens had sky-rocketed in recent years.

She had just removed the sheets from the typewriter and was clipping them neatly with a paperclip when Celia returned with an elegant silver tray set with dainty china cups and saucers. There were tiny sandwiches and chocolate biscuits on plates.

'Oh, you've done it, Lucy,' she beamed. 'So well typed, too. I could never have made such a good job of it. Now, sit down, my dear. I want to talk to you a little . . . about the children, as a matter of fact. Is it one lump or two?'

'Two, please,' said Lucy, with composure.

'Such a good figure you have, too,' laughed Celia lightly. 'I can only have lemon, I'm afraid.'

Lucy smiled as she took the cup, and accepted a small sandwich. She was determined not to let Celia disturb her, and ate the sandwich with obvious enjoyment.

'By the way, when is it your day off?' asked Celia.

'Tomorrow.'

'Ah, tomorrow.' Celia mused for a short while. 'And you planned to take the children out?'

'Only to see Nanny Campbell,' said Lucy, quietly, looking Celia straight in the eye.

'Ah yes. Well, unfortunately I don't think I can manage tomorrow after all. But I would like to borrow them on Saturday if I may . . . take them to the seaside or somewhere. It would be nice if you could come, too, Lucy, but the object of the outing is really for me to get used to handling the boys, on my own.'

'Used to handling them?'

Lucy began to feel slightly bewildered.

'I don't know if Fergus has told you, but we plan to marry soon,' Celia told her happily. 'Another cup, Lucy?'

'Yes, please,' she said mechanically, seeing a hint of malice beginning to creep into Celia's eyes.

'Yes. It will be very quiet . . . only the family on both sides. We've waited such a long time, you see.'

Lucy nodded. It had puzzled her a little that Fergus and Celia had waited so long. Surely there must have been ample opportunity for them to marry many times.

'Fergus was determined to get the shop on its feet, though, after Stuart left.'

'On its feet?' asked Lucy.

It had looked decidedly prosperous to her, and had always been so. No one had ever doubted that Carrick's was anything else but on its feet.

'Of course, my dear, after such a setback.'

'Then Stuart was important to Carrick's?' asked Lucy.

Celia laughed.

'Oh, darling, surely you know all about it,' she said, with amusement, 'though it puzzled me a little bit at first that the Carricks were willing to have you under their roof, after what happened. However, when Fergus explained, I could see the sense in it.'

'Explained what?' asked Lucy, her eyes now wide with curiosity, and an odd feeling of apprehension. Celia knew something, something which was going to hurt her. She could sense it, and felt herself tensing to face it.

'Explained what?' she repeated.

'Why they've kept you at High Crest, of course. You must know that when Stuart and Angela eloped, they didn't go empty-handed.'

'Whatever do you mean?' whispered Lucy.

'So you don't know!' cried Celia. 'You poor dear! I don't think it's fair to have kept you in the dark, though it isn't much fun to know your sister is a thief . . . '

'A thief?' cried Lucy, her limbs beginning to tremble.

'Yes, old Mr Carrick . . . Uncle Tom . . . was alive then, and he had brought a great deal of money home and put it in the safe. He was planning to expand the business and had some sort of cash deal in hand. He had a thing about paying in cash, and getting a good bargain. Stuart and Angela helped themselves to the lot.'

'I don't believe it,' cried Lucy hotly. 'Even if it were true, why blame Angela? Wasn't Stuart capable of taking it? He's been capable of plenty of other things since they married.'

'Now that's interesting,' said Celia softly. 'But in this case, it was dear Angela who was behind it all. Stuart's soft, my dear. He's like a piece of pliable clay. Angela decided they were entitled to a share in the business if they were pulling out, and worked out a plan for Stuart to help himself . . . or rather, to help both of them.'

'How do you know all this?' asked Lucy, her cheeks beginning to glow with colour.

'Because she was a fool, Lucy dear. They were both fools. She wrote it all down in a letter for Stuart, working out the details for him to follow, and telling him to burn the letter. Only he didn't. He'd never have remembered all her detailed instructions, so he kept it. He did it in a book he was reading at the time. It was a book of poems by T. S. Eliot . . . my book, Lucy dear.'

Lucy waited while Celia poured

herself more tea, then sat back complacently.

'I got it back from Fergus after they'd eloped. And guess what! I found the letter.'

'And you gave it to Fergus?' whispered Lucy.

'I did better than that. I took it over one evening and gave it to all three. I was brokenhearted, you see, because of Stuart's treatment of me, but Fergus was there, and worth ten Stuarts. He's probably worth twenty now. You agree with me, don't you, Lucy?'

She flushed and avoided the older girl's eyes.

'I thought you did,' said Celia, smiling a little.

'What . . . what happened then?' Lucy's lips were stiff.

'Oh, poor Fergus had a very bad time,' said Celia, shaking her head. 'Poor old Uncle Tom died, and the money Stuart and Angela took made a big hole in the business. But few people knew about it, and Fergus worked all day and every day to right the ship, as it were. He might even have wanted another career, but he had to stick to the shop; and it's only in recent months that it's all straight again. Of course, we couldn't marry. Fergus wouldn't have wanted me to marry a poor man, would he? He's so proud, you see, though he often took my advice. I'm a good business woman, and I helped him plan the new layout of the shop. He showed it to you, didn't he? He's very proud of it now, you know.'

'Yes, he showed it to me,' said Lucy.

'So you see, he hasn't much love to spare for the Abbotts, nor has Aunt Caroline. Even in Canada, they were soon broke, and Fergus had to pay off their debts.'

'That isn't true!' cried Lucy. '*I*'ve been helping Angela, when Stuart spent all their money, all his earnings on gambling . . . '

'Oh, no!' scoffed Celia. 'I could well believe he'd have a bet on now and again, but I know who was most likely to spend their money, my dear. Leopards don't change their spots so easily. So she's been milking you, too, has she?'

Celia shook her head in admiration.

'You've got to hand it to Angela Abbott,' she said. 'She's quite a girl!'

Lucy was silent, remembering the pitiful, heartbreaking letters. Was Celia right? Or was she telling her a tissue of lies about Angela? Why hadn't the Carricks shown her the door? They must hate her, if all this was true. She caught her breath. Perhaps they *did* hate her.

'Why did they keep me on?' she asked fearfully.

Celia shrugged.

'To keep an eye on you, of course,' she said offhandedly. 'You're an Abbott. They can control what's spent on the children if they're under their own roof, and see what you're up to. They don't want big bills coming in from traders all over Newton Stephens, do they?'

'How dare you!' cried Lucy, jumping to her feet.

'Sit down,' ordered Celia, 'and listen to me! Angela and Stuart will need a fairly long convalescence and Fergus and Caroline may be saddled with those children for months. Why keep you on, when I can do the job just as well? Fergus will keep you on till we're married, then you'll do us all a favour if you take yourself off back to London. You've no moral claim on those children, not after the way Angela nearly ruined Carrick's. You understand?'

Lucy nodded, her eyes enormous in her small white face.

'I've no need to tell you that I can wield . . . certain power . . . if crossed,' said Celia quietly. 'I therefore advise you to pay attention to me. There's no need to make a change until it's necessary. Just remember, though . . . I don't mind you getting your hooks on the children. They can be little hooligans when they like, anyway. But

168

Fergus is nothing to you. He might have some sort of perverse interest in you. Why do we laugh at tragedy, and cry with delight? Just see that's all it is.'

'There's no need for your threats . . . or your blackmail,' said Lucy.

Her voice felt thick and strained, and her limbs were leaden.

'Good afternoon, Miss Grange,' she said politely, and picked up her bag.

'Don't take it too badly, darling,' laughed Celia. 'You might even be useful, if you behave.'

Her laughter followed Lucy, as she walked, stumblingly, up the gravel drive to the main road, and turned again towards High Crest. But it no longer felt like home.

★   ★   ★

The old house was quiet that evening after the children had gone to bed, and Mrs Carrick had supper in her room, deciding that she felt over-tired and wanted to go to bed early.

Lucy carried out her duties mechanically, her mind full of the things Celia Grange had told her. Was her sister really a thief, or was Celia distorting the facts to suit her own ends? She needn't have bothered, thought Lucy despondently, if her object was to keep her and Fergus apart. He took little notice of her when he was at home, and she was glad he was away at present.

Lucy had turned over in her mind all that she knew about her sister. If Celia was right, then all the letters she'd received from Angela were lies. How could she believe a stranger, a girl with an axe to grind even if it were all imaginary, before her own sister?

For a wild moment she'd wanted to go and talk to Mrs Carrick about it. She knew the old lady well enough now to realize she'd be told exactly what happened.

'You know nothing about it,' she had said, when Lucy accused her of insulting Angela. Lucy bit her lip. That seemed to indicate that Celia was telling the truth, unless some terrible mistake had been made. Yet she couldn't ask Mrs Carrick. Every day the old lady seemed to grow quieter and more frail, and she knew that Fergus was worried about his mother. There was no need to add to her burdens.

Lucy's head ached as she lay, sleepless, during the night, turning everything over in her mind. She was glad she was going to Nanny's the following day, and wondered how much Nanny knew. But suppose she knew nothing? To ask her would only add to her worries, too.

Lucy thought of Fergus working day and night to right the business he loved after her sister had all but ruined it for him, and her own fierce independence rose in revolt. If it were true, she wanted to pay it all back . . . but the sum mentioned was far too great. The money she had in the bank, her small nest-egg which was her share of the money her father left, would only pay back a tiny portion.

And she was still accepting their bounty, she thought miserably. They were still supporting the children, and herself, in food and clothing. Lucy's cheeks burned when she remembered the tightening of Mrs Carrick's mouth when she wrote out the generous cheque for the children's clothing. No wonder the old lady had been angry when she saw how poorly clad they were.

After breakfast she dressed the children and took them to see their grandmother before leaving for Nanny's.

'They are looking well, my dear,' the old lady told her, and Lucy was glad to see that Mrs Carrick, too, was looking well. 'You're doing a good job in looking after them.'

Lucy felt a lump in her throat. She would have felt better if Mrs Carrick had been in a haughty mood, and had made one of her tart comments. But the bright black eyes were gentle, then thoughtful as she looked at the young girl.

'You look tired, Lucy,' she said kindly. 'I don't wonder. Although I love my grandsons dearly, they can be tiring at times. Perhaps I could arrange for you to have a few days off.'

Lucy shook her head. She would never resolve her problems by running away from them.

'I'm all right,' she said, with a small smile. 'Just a headache. It will be gone when I get to Airlie Cottage. Kiss Grandmother, boys, and let's go now. We must catch the bus.'

Nanny Campbell, too, was concerned when she saw Lucy's white face and dark-circled eyes.

'Och, you look worn to bits, Miss Lucy,' she said, impatiently. 'You've been doing far too much. Anybody can see that. Ye've been letting these two lead you by the nose. I always say a wee skelp now and again does no harm at a'.'

Lucy smiled broadly.

'How often did you skelp me?' she asked mischievously.

'Enough, enough . . . and maybe not enough in other quarters,' Nanny retorted darkly.

'Oh, Nanny,' cried Lucy, 'was . . . was Angela really naughty when she was growing up?'

Nanny pursed her lips, realizing there was more behind the question than Lucy's usual lighthearted talk of childhood days.

'She was a bit spoiled, Miss Lucy,' she said at length, 'and I'm as much to blame as anybody. She was aye such a bonny wee lass wi' lovely fair curls and big blue eyes. She was the only one, too, till she was seven and you came along. Maybe that's why your parents doted on her, an' she got all her own way. But she's older now, and I dare say she'll have outgrown all that. She was still just a bairn when she went away.'

But old enough to know right from wrong, thought Lucy, sadly. Her head still ached, and the boys were beginning to quarrel again, their active minds needing something to do. She took them out into the large back garden of the cottage, and found them a corner of the garden where they could play with their small buckets and spades.

'I think I'll lie down for a while, Nanny,' she said. 'My head aches a little.'

'I thocht ye were brewing up one of your headaches,' said Nanny. 'You go straight up to bed, and I'll see to the children. Don't worry about a thing.'

Lucy was glad to crawl between the lavender-scented sheets. She loved her pretty attic bedroom, but even that seemed alien now, since she'd found out the Granges were the real owners of Nanny's cottage. Her head throbbed dully, and her throat ached.

Some time later she woke up as a cool hand caressed her forehead, and she saw Martin smiling down at her, with Nanny hovering in the background.

'Hello, Martin,' she whispered. 'Oh,

Nanny, you needn't have sent for him. I'm O.K. really.'

'You've caught a very nasty cold,' he said firmly. 'Nanny was quite right. I'm leaving some tablets for you, and I'll be back tomorrow. We'll talk then.'

Lucy nodded heavily. She did feel under the weather, and watched Martin usher Nanny out of the bedroom, hearing his pleasant voice as they walked downstairs. From somewhere she could hear the children shouting, and hoped that Nanny would come back soon so that she could ask a few questions.

'They're playing fine,' she was told, when Nanny did come back.

'I wish we were on the phone,' mumbled Lucy. 'I'll have to let Mrs Carrick know I'm staying here tonight.'

'And what's to stop me ringing from the Post Office?' asked Nanny. 'It's only a minute's walk up the road.'

'Oh, would you?' asked Lucy gratefully. 'I wouldn't like to worry her at the moment. She gets tired easily.'

Nanny put on her old brown coat and took the children by the hand. The Post Office was one of their favourite shops, having a liberal supply of sweets on display. Ten minutes later Lucy heard them returning, and Nanny again climbed the stairs.

'I left a message,' she said, a trifle breathlessly. 'It was Miss Grange. She said she'd tell Mrs Carrick.'

Lucy looked curiously at Nanny's face.

'You don't like Celia Grange, do you, Nanny?' she asked.

The old lady pursed her lips.

'I've got to lump Miss Grange,' she said, 'whether I like it or not.'

Lucy nodded, knowing now that the report she had typed had been a correct one. Mr Grange was Nanny's landlord.

A good peaceful sleep did wonders for Lucy, and Martin called next day, and was obviously pleased with her progress.

'You can get up tomorrow,' he said, smiling. 'It's Saturday, and I won't be so busy. I want to talk to you, as a matter of fact, so I'll arrange for a little bit of free time. See you tomorrow, my dear.'

'All right, Martin,' she said gratefully.

'He's really rather nice,' she said to Nanny, when she returned after seeing the doctor out.

'Aye, but young doctors these days are still no' like the auld ones . . . your father, for instance. They aye seem in sich a hurry. Dr Steele stays to speak to you because he admires you, Miss Lucy, but when auld Mrs Macrae had the 'flu, and I went in to gie her a wee bit help, he was in and out like a whirlwind. There's no' the same patience these days or . . . or love. Your father fair loved his patients.'

Lucy nodded. She probably saw Martin at his best, but she could well imagine him being impatient if it suited him.

Next day, however, she felt so much better that it was fun to see him again. Nanny had taken the boys for a short walk, and she was in by herself, leisurely tidying up the usually immaculate house. Nanny had found quite a variety of old toys for the children, and now they littered the room.

She opened the door to Martin with a welcoming smile, and he came in breezily, his keen eyes sweeping over her.

'That's better,' he beamed. 'More like my old Lucy.'

'Your tablets worked wonders, doctor,' she told him, dimpling.

'I've other things I can recommend,' he told her, taking her hand. 'Do you feel well enough to come out with me this evening? There's quite a good play on at the theatre.'

Lucy bit her lip. The truth was that she didn't really want to go out with Martin again. Yet he was young, and she had so few young people to talk to at the moment. If only she could have confided in him over Angela, but she could well imagine the horror on his face if he knew how the Carricks really regarded their daughter-in-law. Lucy shrewdly suspected that a great deal of her attraction lay in the fact that the Carricks appeared to have accepted her as one of the family.

She sighed, realizing that she and Martin would never really be true friends. They were poles apart.

'I'm sorry, Martin,' she said gently. 'I'd rather not.'

'But why?' he broke in impatiently. 'You look a hundred per cent fit again.'

'But Nanny doesn't,' answered Lucy. 'She's tired, Martin, having had the twins here all this time, and being in charge of them. She's no longer young, you know, and I must see to them myself this evening.'

'Oh, all right,' said Martin sulkily, though seeing the logic of this. 'I'll ask you again after you return to High Crest, shall I?'

'Of course,' she smiled.

There was no need to hurt him, she decided, and he'd soon realize that her feelings for him would never go beyond friendship, and she'd meant it when she told him so before.

She saw him to the door, smiling and waving until he was out of sight. A moment later, as she was about to go into the cottage, another car slid to a stop at the gate. Lucy caught her breath and stood stock-still as Fergus slowly climbed from the driving seat and walked deliberately towards her, up the path. As he drew near she saw that his face was a mask of anger.

'You little fool!' he greeted her. 'How dare you remove the children from High Crest, and bring them here, without a word? How dare you! And how dare you break your promise to me, and worry my mother when she's had enough burdens already? Get the children immediately, and collect your own things. I have too much to do to waste time arguing.'

Lucy felt as though she had been slapped. What did he mean . . . without a word? Nanny had phoned, hadn't she? Surely Celia wouldn't withhold the message? Fergus was now striding round the empty cottage, looking at the scattered toys.

'They . . . they aren't here,' she stammered. 'Nanny has them out for a walk.'

'Oh!'

Fergus picked up an old teddybear which had been her own, and threw it down again. His eyes smouldered broodingly.

'So you couldn't stick High Crest any longer,' he said heavily. 'You had to run away. Well, you'll be glad to know it isn't going to last much longer. The children's parents are already on their way home, and may even have arrived by now. Angela will be confined to bed for a little while longer, but Stuart is able to get about with a stick.' His lip curled a little. 'I've left word for Steele to call. He'll probably be dancing attendance on your sister every day, so there'll be no need to sneak away to meet him. I passed his car a moment ago, so I see that he at least mustn't be kept in the dark over your plans.'

Lucy's head was whirling. She could see that Fergus was enraged, and had no idea how to tell him the truth without it appearing like another excuse. Her mind had mainly managed to grasp the most important detail. Angela was on her way home, and might even now be at High Crest, as she listened to Fergus telling her the arrangements he had made for picking them up at the airport.

Now Lucy was trembling visibly at the thought of seeing her sister again so soon. Fergus looked at her, the anger leaving his face as he brushed a hand across his forehead, rather wearily.

'Stop shaking,' he commanded her. 'I suppose I shouldn't have lost my temper so violently, only . . . only I suppose I was disappointed. I forgot you're so young.'

He looked at her, and Lucy wished she could find the right words to explain. She would have preferred his anger to this resignation which would probably lead to indifference.

'Nanny left a message,' she began. 'She rang . . . '

'Uncle Fergus! Uncle Fergus!'

She was interrupted by the arrival of the twins, with Nanny breathlessly bringing up the rear.

'You know Mr Carrick, don't you, Nanny?' asked Lucy. 'Mrs Campbell looked after us when we were children.'

'Hello, Nanny,' smiled Fergus, and Lucy felt a lump in her throat when she saw the gentleness in his smile, and his delight at seeing the boys again. They had caught him in a strangling hug, and he sat down hurriedly on the carpet, grinning boyishly.

'Ye'll be wanting to take them back, Mr Fergus. Will ye be stopping for tea first?'

'No time,' said Fergus. 'Sorry, Nanny. If Lucy will get the things we'll go now. The children's parents are on their way home.'

184

'That's a mercy,' said Nanny fervently. 'That's the best news I've had for a while.'

Fergus nodded, and turned to Lucy who arrived with the coats and a shopping bag.

'They don't need those,' he said. 'We'll put them in the boot. Come on, kids. Back seat for you two. Kiss Nanny goodbye.'

'Cheerio, Nanny,' whispered Lucy. 'See you soon.'

'Look after yourself, my lamb,' Nanny told her. 'Don't go getting yourself ill again.'

'What did she mean, ill?' asked Fergus as she climbed into the car.

'Oh, nothing much,' Lucy told him tiredly. She'd lost all interest in explanations, and now she only wanted to see Angela again. She must get to know her sister, and judge for herself what kind of person she was. And some time, when Angela was quite well again, she would find out the real truth.

7

When they arrived back at High Crest, Lucy could see at once that the house was in turmoil. Doors were wide open, luggage in the hall, and Nessie Cree came hurrying out to meet them.

'Mr Stuart's home,' she said excitedly. 'Mrs Stuart, too . . . your sister, Miss Lucy. Madam is in the big sitting-room with them. Poor Mr Stuart is walking with a stick, and Mrs Stuart is resting on a settee.'

Lucy hardly heard her. With a twin on either hand, she walked into the sitting-room, pausing on the threshold. Then it seemed as though the years rolled away as her sister turned to greet her, and once again she was looking into Angela's beautiful face, her tumbling fair hair slightly disarranged, but her lovely blue eyes shining with welcome.

'Angela,' whispered Lucy, and ran to hug her. 'Oh, I'm so glad to see you!'

'Well, you *have* grown up, darling,' said Angela, a faint Canadian accent overlying her soft Scottish voice. 'It's so lovely to see you again.'

'It's wonderful, truly wonderful,' cried Lucy, and looked with love and pride at her beautiful sister, a feeling of overwhelming relief sweeping over her. Angela had been well named. In spite of her long weeks in hospital, she looked delicately lovely, her eyes soft and innocent. It was difficult to believe that anyone could ever accuse her of anything despicable. Celia Grange had distorted the facts out of all recognition, thought Lucy angrily.

'Well, dear, is it really me?' asked Angela, softly, and Lucy blushed, aware that she had been staring.

'Don't I get introduced to my sister-in-law?'

Lucy turned as a tall, very thin man rose from a chair, and limped towards her, smiling. Mrs Carrick had been sitting beside him, smiling proudly, but it was Fergus who made the introductions.

'Of course,' he said. 'Lucy, my dear, your brother-in-law, Stuart.'

He was older-looking than Fergus, and very like him, though his face was gentler, and perhaps a trifle weak. But his dark eyes sparkled with kindness and good humour, even though the lines of suffering were clearly marked round the mouth. Lucy decided she liked him, and smiled as she held out her hand.

'Hello, Stuart,' she said shyly, and he bent and kissed her cheek.

'Thank you for looking after the twins,' he said, and she turned to look for them. They were standing just behind her, looking slightly bewildered and rather frightened.

'Why, darlings,' cried Lucy, 'haven't you got a hug for your mummy and daddy?'

They hung back for a second longer, but it was Stuart to whom they rushed, burying their small faces in his jacket.

'Daddy! Daddy!' cried Ian, and Lucy felt her eyes grow moist, and watched Fergus turn away.

'Mummy's turn now,' said Stuart. 'Give Mummy a kiss.'

Obediently they rushed to Angela, who hugged them to her with a small sob.

'Hello, darlings,' she said huskily. 'I can hardly believe you're both here. And how you've grown! Haven't they grown, Stuart?'

He nodded, and they ran to him again.

'Up, Daddy!' cried David. 'Up! Up!'

Stuart's face sobered, and he smiled wryly.

'Daddy's got a sore leg,' he explained gently. 'Not up just yet, my lad.'

Mrs Carrick caught Lucy's eye.

'I think it's time for tea anyway,' she said. 'Go with Aunt Lucy, boys, and have your faces and hands washed. Mummy and Daddy will see you later.'

Nessie had prepared the big main

bedroom for Stuart and Angela. It had been old Mr Carrick's bedroom, but when he died, Mrs Carrick had preferred something smaller at the back of the house. Fergus, too, had preferred to keep the bedroom which had been his since he was a boy.

'I think the main bedroom will be best, since Angela will have to stay in bed for a short time yet. It's straight along from the nursery, and you'll be able to see the children, my dear.'

'Thank you, Mrs Carrick,' said Angela. 'I like lots of room.'

'I will carry her up,' offered Fergus, 'if you'll permit me.'

'Thank you,' said Angela again composedly, and Fergus picked her up as though she were a feather.

'I shall see you later, Angela,' said Mrs Carrick. 'There's quite a lot we must discuss.'

For the first time a flush stained the girl's pale cheeks.

'All right,' she said huskily. 'I'd like to see Lucy, too, when she's free.'

190

* ★ ★

When Lucy had put the children to bed, she went along to the large main bedroom where Angela was now in bed. The room had a fire, in spite of the warmth of the summer evening, and Angela was propped up against lace-trimmed pillows, looking rather like a princess in a fairy tale.

The room was richly furnished with elegant highly-polished furniture, and Lucy looked round with appreciation.

'Are you comfortable, Angela?' she asked, sitting down on a small gold-brocaded chair near the bed.

'Very,' said Angela complacently.

'I . . . I'm sorry I didn't manage to keep the children myself, as you asked,' said Lucy hesitantly, but Angela waved her hand airily.

'Stuart's idea to send them here was the right one,' she said airily. 'I forgot the old girl would be sure to take to her grandchildren.'

For a moment Lucy felt chilled.

'But of course she loves her grand-children. Mrs Carrick has been very good to them . . . and to me.'

'Fine,' said Angela heartily. 'Now tell me all about everyone here.'

'There isn't much to tell really,' said Lucy slowly. 'I take the children to see Mrs Carrick every day. Fer . . . Fergus is usually away all day at business.'

She tried to keep the warm colour out of her cheeks when she talked about Fergus, but was aware of Angela's close scrutiny.

'Then . . . then there's Nessie Cree, the housekeeper. She helps me with the children sometimes . . . and Rose, a young local girl who only comes part-time.'

'I see,' said Angela. 'Not a very big staff.'

'I believe Fergus found business . . . difficult, for a little while,' said Lucy, watching Angela's face. But again there was no sign of guilt on the lovely features, and she relaxed a little with relief. Angela was absolutely innocent . . . she was sure of that.

'They're still a great deal wealthier than we could ever be,' said Angela, stroking the rich eiderdown on her bed. 'Anyone else?'

'Only Miss Grange,' said Lucy, as casually as she could. 'She's away on holiday at the moment.'

'Celia Grange?' asked Angela sharply.

'Yes . . . she's going to marry Fergus,' said Lucy flatly.

'The more fool him,' said Angela, 'unless she's greatly changed.'

Lucy bit her lip.

'I . . . I don't think she has, Angela,' she said, hesitantly. 'She . . . well, I don't think she'll be very nice to you.'

'She hates me,' said Angela simply, and Lucy nodded. Celia must hate Angela, but surely she couldn't do her very much harm. After all, Angela was now a Carrick, a member of this family.

Suddenly Angela lay back and stretched out her arms luxuriously, then began to laugh almost hysterically.

'Isn't it funny, Lucy?' she asked.

'Don't you think it's funny?'

'What is?' asked Lucy, bewildered.

'My being here . . . in the best bedroom, too. You don't know how funny it is.'

'I don't know what you mean,' said Lucy, her blue eyes wide and puzzled, and a small stab of fear in her heart.

'Oh, never mind, darling. Just a little joke. Are you going now? I think I'd like a rest.'

'Of course. Goodnight, Angela.'

Lucy stood up.

'Will you be able to do little errands for me . . . in between looking after the children . . . since there's no proper maid?' asked Angela sleepily.

'Of course,' said Lucy again, then went quietly out of the room, feeling not a little uneasy. She should feel very close to her only sister, she thought, even if they had been parted for seven years. But there had been moments when Angela had seemed like a stranger to her.

'You're looking thoughtful,' said

Fergus, and she started guiltily. 'Not making plans for running away from us again?'

She flushed.

'My sister's going to need me,' she said quietly, 'and so are the children as yet. I shan't be running out on my responsibilities.'

'No?' he asked lightly, then added quietly. 'Don't go slaving yourself for Angela's sake, Lucy.'

'I wouldn't dream of it,' she told him. 'I shall help her all I can, though. That won't be slaving.'

'Won't it?' asked Fergus in the same sceptical tone, and Lucy turned to face him.

'I'm glad they've come home,' she said proudly. 'It will maybe give you and Mrs Carrick a chance to get to know Angela better, and stop all this resentment. You'll find out for yourselves just how nice and sweet she is.'

'I'm glad, too, Lucy, for similar reasons,' said Fergus softly. 'Let's hope neither of us will be disappointed, my dear.'

'Goodnight,' she whispered, as she slipped past him.

'Goodnight, Lucy,' said Fergus, and her throat tightened at the gentleness in his tone.

★ ★ ★

Martin called to see Angela next morning. Lucy had already told her sister that the doctor was coming to see her, and the tell-tale colour again rose in her cheeks.

'Who is he?' asked Angela curiously.

'Martin Steele. As a matter of fact, we've been friends,' said Lucy.

'Just friends?'

She nodded.

'I'm not in love with him, Angela, and I'm sure he doesn't really love me, but he's a good companion. We've been to concerts . . . that sort of thing.'

'Sounds a bit dull, darling,' said Angela.

'Perhaps I'm a dull person,' said Lucy lightly, though this morning she didn't look dull, thought Angela, through narrowed eyelids. The morning sun caught her dark curls and seemed to spark them with dark blue lights, which contrasted vividly with her violety-blue eyes. Lucy was really very much prettier than she'd imagined the previous evening.

Lucy was allowed to remain in the bedroom when Martin examined her sister, and she winced at the long, angry-looking red scars which were on her sister's legs, and which showed up vividly against the whiteness of her skin.

'Mainly your right leg,' said Martin, and Angela nodded.

'Your husband's left,' he said again thoughtfully. 'Who was driving?'

'He was,' said Angela shortly. 'Does it matter?'

Martin pursed his lips, and shook his head.

'Not really. Just interested in how your legs have been trapped, that's all. I think you ought to stay in bed a couple of days to get over the journey, then try getting up. You'll need a stick, of course, but you'll be able to get about pretty much like your husband. Gradually the scars will fade, and you should make an excellent recovery. You've been lucky, Mrs Carrick.'

'So everyone keeps telling me,' said Angela pettishly. 'What they don't say is that we were damned unlucky to crash in the first place.'

'Hm ... yes, there is that,' said Martin, then smiled warmly. 'At least your beauty hasn't been spoiled,' he said cheerfully, and Angela thawed visibly.

'Only a little scar near my ear,' she said, lifting the heavy curtain of pale gold hair. 'It healed quickly.'

'It would have been a shame,' said Martin softly, then turned briskly to Lucy. 'I'll be back tomorrow, my dear,' he said. 'Just to keep an eye on my patient. How about you? I was surprised to find you away from Nanny

Campbell's cottage.'

'I had to come back here,' said Lucy quickly, as they walked downstairs together. 'Angela had come home, you see.'

'Of course,' said Martin, 'but don't overdo things, will you? Perhaps we could have that date I asked you for one evening soon?'

'That would be nice,' said Lucy, 'but I . . . er . . . I shall have to see. I may not be free.'

Martin nodded non-committally, and went off to speak to Mrs Carrick. Lucy sighed and ran back up to Angela's room to see her settled with some magazines, before going to find the twins.

Lucy would have found her task rather difficult if she hadn't had Stuart's help. Nessie Cree had grown rather huffy, now that Angela was installed in the best bedroom, and was demanding special delicacies on a tray, and she complained rather bitterly to Lucy and Mrs Carrick.

'I know she's your sister, Miss Lucy, and Mr Stuart's wife, but she's a thrawn lass, nevertheless. She's fair fu' o' wants, wanting this an' wanting that. This isn't good for her, and she doesn't like that. She's got me fair fed up, I can tell you.'

Lucy glanced quickly at Mrs Carrick, whose face was as impassive as ever.

'Angela suffered a great deal of pain, Nessie,' she defended her. 'Maybe she's entitled to be a bit difficult. I'll try to do more for her, and relieve you.'

'You've got quite enough to do already,' said Mrs Carrick briefly. 'Will you send Rose to me when she comes in? We can't really afford more staff, Nessie, and good girls are hard to get, but maybe Rose would manage to come more often. I believe she's a good worker, Nessie?'

'She's all right,' mumbled Nessie, but still looked aggrieved. She wouldn't have minded the extra work, but that Angela always managed to get her back up.

'She'll be up in a couple of days,' said Lucy soothingly. 'That should make things better, Nessie.'

'Aye, all right,' agreed Nessie, and made her way back to the kitchen.

Lucy found Stuart playing with his sons in the nursery. Now that she'd time to talk to him, she could see the lines of suffering on his face, and felt a wave of sympathy for him.

'That game was a bit too strenuous, chaps,' he said, flopping into a chair, while the two small boys rushed towards him.

'Sit down on your own little chairs,' commanded Lucy, 'beside Daddy, and you can have your orange juice and biscuits. Your daddy and I are having coffee.'

As she settled them and turned her attention to Stuart, she found him regarding her intently.

'You aren't at all like Angela,' he said at length, and she laughed and coloured.

'No, not much. She was like Mother,

but I take after Father. Angela got all the looks.'

'Not all,' corrected Stuart thoughtfully. 'We'll have to get to know each other, Lucy, since we're related. I've been looking at some of the books you have here. Fond of reading?'

'Very,' she told him. 'I loved going to see Carrick's. Fergus took me, and I thought it a wonderful bookseller's.'

'It *is* wonderful,' said Stuart quietly, and she was surprised at the sudden whitening of his face, and the pain in his eyes.

'You've . . . missed it?' she asked gently.

'For years it was my life,' he told her, 'but I didn't know I loved it until it was too late.'

'Have you had — regrets, then?' asked Lucy carefully, and Stuart's eyes went to his two small sons, caressing their curly heads.

'Of course not,' he said with a smile. 'There is much I have to regret, but there are always compensations.'

'A wife and family?' she asked, laughing. 'Dependants?'

'Dependants,' he agreed.

'Did you like Canada?' she pursued, and again Stuart paused for thought.

'In some ways it was delightful. It was a challenge . . . something to appeal to youth . . . something to incite one to take risks, to overcome obstacles, if you know what I mean. Angela . . . Angela didn't settle down too well, though. She found some of the shops . . . er . . . expensive.'

'But you had several jobs?' pursued Lucy, and again Stuart smiled wryly.

'Yes,' he agreed briefly. 'More than several. I had many jobs. If you ever want to test your own character, my dear, then just emigrate. You'll get to know yourself very well, and find out what you're really worth.'

The bitter twist to his mouth saddened her.

'But you must have gained a lot of experience,' she said consolingly.

'A lot of experience,' agreed Stuart,

then turned to smile at the children who were growing restless. 'What do they do now?' he asked.

'Oh, we usually go for our morning walk,' said Lucy. 'Like to come, or would it be too much for you?'

'I think it would be the best thing possible for me,' grinned Stuart. 'I'll have to get this old leg exercised somehow.'

'Will you feel nervous about driving again?' she asked, as she slipped on the children's cardigans.

'I think I'll feel more nervous being Angela's passenger again,' he laughed, and she frowned.

'But Angela said you were driving,' she told him, looking at him curiously.

'Oh, of course,' he replied briefly. 'Coming, chaps?'

The twins made a great deal of noise finding their balls and the small toys which were allowed. Lucy had placed a limit on the things they could take, after being weighed down one day with large cumbersome toys.

'I'll take Daddy's hand,' cried Ian.

'No, I'll take it,' protested David.

'Ian will take it going, and David coming back,' said Lucy. 'Come on, David.'

Stuart looked at her with respect.

'You're good at managing them, Lucy,' he told her.

'I've had to be!' she assured him.

* * *

'You're very friendly with Stuart, aren't you, Lucy?' asked Angela, obviously trying to be offhand.

'I like him,' said Lucy. 'You know, Angela, he may have been a little irresponsible in the past, according to what you used to tell me in your letters ... and what I've heard from other quarters ... but I do think he's different now. In many ways he's very like Fergus, and well able to shoulder his responsibilities. When he's quite better, of course.'

'Hm.' Angela was non-committal.

'Maybe the accident has done that,' went on Lucy, as she tidied the bedroom. 'Maybe it's made him think twice about himself and his family. Such a thing often happens, you know.'

Angela's eyes were veiled and she said nothing, then she slid down on to the pillows and closed her eyes.

'I've got a headache, Lucy,' she said, rather tiredly. 'Just leave me for half an hour, and I'll be O.K.'

'Sure you don't want anything?'

'Quite sure.'

A day or two later Angela decided she'd try to get up, and it seemed as though she'd shed all her pettiness and ill-temper when she left the large, rather sombre bedroom, and came downstairs to sit in the lounge. She seemed determined to be charming and helpful to everyone, and gradually the old house settled down into a new routine, with tensions eased and a spirit of unity all round.

Nessie Cree had less to complain about, and went about her work with her usual cheerful bustle. Stuart spent more and more time looking after the children, while Angela quietly read books which Fergus brought home for her, and occasionally wound wool for old Mrs Carrick, who enjoyed knitting socks for Fergus which he wore faithfully during the winter months.

Now and again Angela and Mrs Carrick found a subject of common interest, and held animated conversations, but sometimes the old lady preferred to sit quietly in her own small study, instead of joining in with the family. She was looking less tired these days, and obviously happy to have Stuart home again.

Lucy hardly noticed that she had a great deal to do. She was happy, and so relieved that the Carricks had now come to know Angela and accept her as one of themselves. Lucy had not been completely settled in her mind until she'd talked over Celia's accusations with her sister, but she now knew that they had been greatly exaggerated and distorted.

'Do you believe her?' Angela asked, her large blue eyes very serious.

'No, I don't,' said Lucy firmly.

Angela sighed, and took her sister's hand.

'We did take our fares, I'm afraid,' she confessed, 'but it was Stuart's own money. It was only some commission which was due to him, and he was entitled to that.'

'That's all right,' said Lucy, with understanding. 'I knew it must only be something of the sort. I mean, you couldn't come here and allow the Carricks to look after you all, if you'd stolen money from them and nearly ruined the business.'

'Ruined the business? How ridiculous,' said Angela. 'Of course we couldn't have come back under those circumstances.'

Lucy was satisfied, glad to be able to look Fergus and Mrs Carrick in the face. She was happy to run errands for Angela, in between looking after the children and giving Nessie a hand with the evening meal. She felt tired occasionally, but had no idea that her eyes had grown large and darkly shadowed in her small face, until Martin suddenly looked closely at her one day, after calling in to see Angela.

'Your sister is doing fine,' he told her. 'She's walking well with her sticks, and might even manage to do without it before Stuart. But you look tired, Lucy. What did you do on your last day off? Go and see Nanny?'

Lucy coloured.

'I haven't really bothered about time off for a week or two,' she said evasively. 'There's been no real need.'

'There's every need,' said Martin. 'I've got to drive to Stranraer on Saturday afternoon, on business. I shall call for you at two o'clock. That's doctor's orders, Lucy.'

She smiled ruefully.

'Very well, doctor.'

The weather was still nice, and she'd enjoy driving to Stranraer, she thought, happily. Besides, she and Martin seemed to have reached a new understanding, that she wanted no more than his friendship. This seemed to suit Martin quite well. He was the type of man to stay away from marriage until he was well established, then allow his head to choose him a wife. Lucy knew he was, perhaps, more fond of her than he'd been of any girl, but his feelings didn't go very deep over anything. This was perhaps part of his success as a doctor.

★ ★ ★

On Friday afternoon Lucy was hurrying home loaded with shopping, when she bumped into Fergus at the front door.

She felt very tired, and could only smile gratefully when he relieved her of her parcels. She'd seen little of him recently, as he seemed to spend a great deal of time at business. So far there had been no plans made for his wedding to Celia, and Lucy remembered this now and again, uneasily. Angela was growing stronger every day, however, and she knew she would be able to make her own plans soon for returning to London.

She was happy in rather a negative sort of way, just having a casual word with Fergus now and again, but after he was married and belonged to someone else, things would be different. Celia wouldn't want her around, and she wouldn't want to be here in any case.

Celia would be home soon from her holiday on the Continent. How would she treat Angela? wondered Lucy. No doubt she'd be very annoyed to find Stuart and his family so much at home in High Crest.

Now as Lucy stumbled up the steps with her packages, Fergus put out a restraining hand.

'Whoa there!' he called. 'Lucy, for heaven's sake, child, is there any need to do so much shopping at the same time? And why don't you get it delivered?'

'It's only some things for Angela,' she panted. 'They're very light, really. Just bulky.'

'It's still too much for you,' he said sincerely, then caught her arm and turned her round to stare into her face.

'You look like a wilting snowdrop,' he told her, 'at Angela's beck and call all day, no doubt. You're so obliging you make me tired. She's perfectly capable of doing almost everything for herself now, you know.'

'I'm not her slave, if that's what you mean,' said Lucy with annoyance. 'She wouldn't make more demands on me than she needs to, and she is doing lots more for herself.'

Fergus glowered at her.

'More like a thistle than a snowdrop,' he commented. 'Always flying to Angela's defence, and if you allow her to make you into her shadow, the more fool you.'

'I'm not anybody's shadow,' she snapped hotly. 'You . . . you make me feel like a doormat!'

'And that's what you could become, quite easily,' said Fergus. 'I wondered how long you'd put up with it before showing a bit of smeddum. Now I'm beginning to wonder if you have any.'

'Leave me alone,' she said tiredly, 'and stop picking on Angela. Surely you all know her well enough by now to see she's a very sweet person. In a way this accident has been a godsend. It's changed things quite a lot.'

Fergus's hard face suddenly softened.

'There I could agree with you, little Lucy,' he said, a very odd note in his voice. She looked at him, rather disconcerted, wondering if he meant that any other way.

'You need a break,' he said gently. 'Be ready tomorrow afternoon, and I'll take you with me to Ayr. Leave the twins with Angela.'

Her eyes shone, then she remembered Martin and flushed a little.

'I'm sorry, Fergus,' she said hesitantly. 'I can't. I'm going to Stranraer with Martin.'

The smile left his eyes and he stared hard at her.

'So it's still Martin, is it?' he asked coldly. 'And I'm worrying about your off-time needlessly. You seem very capable of planning it for yourself. All right then, Lucy. Have a nice day.'

He swung her packages into the hall, then waved briefly as he climbed into his car. Lucy watched him go, her heart heavy with regret. When he stopped criticizing Angela, she enjoyed his companionship so much.

Then she sighed as she walked into the sitting-room. Perhaps it was just as well. It wasn't any fun being in love, and trying to keep it secret from one's beloved. She shrank from the expression in Fergus's eyes if he ever found out her true feelings for him.

8

Next day Lucy dressed for her date with Martin, feeling quite excited with anticipation. She wore a fresh, crisp green and white dress which made her look a little like Fergus's snowdrop, and the prospect of the day ahead lent colour to her cheeks and made her eyes sparkle.

Angela eyed her a little huffily.

'You're all dressed up,' she said coldly. 'Lucky Lucy! Nice to be able to run about and do what you like.'

'You'll be able to do the same shortly, Angela,' Lucy told her happily. 'You know you're almost back to normal now. Why not go with Stuart when he takes the children out?'

'How exciting!' said Angela sarcastically, then smiled with apology when Lucy turned to give her a straight look. 'Sorry, darling. I get a bit sore at times.

Perhaps I will go out with Stuart after all.'

Mrs Carrick looked up from her knitting to give Lucy an approving look.

'How nice you look, my dear,' she complimented, 'and what a good idea for Angela to go out so long as it isn't very far. It's such a lovely day.'

Angela turned away, an impatient look in her eyes.

'It gets so boring at times,' she complained. 'Ah well, mustn't grumble, I suppose. Here's Martin, Lucy. All dolled up in his best suit, too. Sure you aren't eloping?'

'Don't be silly, Angela,' said Lucy, annoyed, and bit her lip to keep from making a more pointed remark.

'Have a nice day, dear,' said Mrs Carrick mildly, though Lucy caught an odd gleam of humour in her eyes as she picked up her white summer coat.

'Thank you,' she said softly, and ran lightly down the steps, her small green sandals twinkling.

It was a glorious day. The coastline

was calm and clear, with small waves breaking against the rocks in milky-white foam. Lucy breathed the fresh sea air, and felt like a bird released from its cage. Not that she was fed up with her family, she assured herself. If it wasn't for Angela, Stuart and the children, she'd have no one of her own at all.

Yet it was good to belong to herself again, and she turned a radiant face to Martin as the breeze whipped her hair into tiny black curls.

'It's lovely to have a break,' she said gratefully. 'Thank you, Martin.'

'It's certainly doing you good,' he agreed. 'You look lovely, my dear. In fact . . . ' He bit his lip. 'We never discussed marriage again, Lucy. Yet you're the one girl with whom I could live happily.'

'I don't think that's so, Martin,' she told him seriously. 'I think you need someone very different from me . . . someone with ambition.'

'But what will you do when Stuart

and Angela go home? That might be soon now.'

'Go back to London. I'm one of those rare creatures who can love Newton Stephens and still love London, too. There's much there that I miss.'

Yet wouldn't it be much more lonely now, she wondered, after belonging to a demanding family? And never to see Fergus again? Suddenly the pleasure in her day began to ebb. It was fun being here with Martin, walking along the waterfront and watching the lovely *Antrim Princess* leave for Ireland, but her heart wasn't in it. She was rather quiet on the journey home, and Martin, too, said little.

'I should have tried a bit harder, shouldn't I, Lucy?' he asked, his voice full of regret, as she hopped lightly out of the car in the soft twilight.

'Wh . . . what do you mean, Martin?' she asked, her eyes questioning.

'Never mind, darling,' he told her. 'It doesn't matter.'

She watched the car go out of sight,

then made her way, slowly, into the house.

Thrown on a chair in the hall was a pale primrose silk coat with matching gloves. Lucy had no difficulty in recognizing it as Celia's, and in any case, her high-pitched voice was coming clearly from the sitting-room.

Lucy walked into the sitting-room to find Celia on her feet, her voice ringing with anger, while Angela sat, white-faced, on the settee. Mrs Carrick was also sitting bolt upright in her favourite chair, her black eyes glittering.

'How dare you lord it over me,' Celia was shouting, 'as though you were the daughter of the house! How dare you even have the effrontery to come here after what you've done! You and Stuart! You've got a nerve trying to tell me what to do . . .'

'Angela has every right to be here,' said Lucy quietly. 'As Stuart's wife, she *is* the daughter of the house.'

She looked at her sister's face, almost transparently pale, and anger began to choke her. Angela had been so much better, yet here was Celia Grange, tanned and healthy-looking from her holiday, doing her best to bully a sick girl. Mrs Carrick, too, was gripping the arm of her chair, but Lucy could see how upset she was, and that her right hand trembled as she began to search for her handkerchief. A few short months ago, she would have shown Celia the door with scant ceremony, Lucy was sure. Even if she was engaged to Fergus, the girl had no right to behave like this.

'But you've no right to come here and upset everyone, Celia,' said Lucy, looking the other girl straight in the eye. 'You've tried to make enough trouble, distorting facts to make my sister and her husband appear to be thieves, and even trying to blackmail me by hinting that my aunt's tenancy of her cottage is insecure, because you own it. But you go too far when you endanger my sister's health. So please go.'

Celia was almost speechless with rage.

'How dare you!' she choked. 'You're almost as bad as she is, willing to accept hand-outs. And what do you mean . . . distorting facts? I've neither distorted nor exaggerated anything. Your sister incited Stuart to help himself to a large sum of money . . . '

'That will do, Celia,' said Mrs Carrick sternly. 'It's a family matter.'

'It's got to be said, Aunt Caroline.' Celia's voice rang out triumphantly. 'They took the firm's ready cash, and if it hadn't been for Fergus, there would be no Carrick's. Deny that if you can!'

She turned to Angela, who was now chalk-white. Lucy looked from one to the other.

'Tell her the truth, Angela,' she said gently. 'Don't be frightened of her, or let her bully you. You know Stuart only took the amount due to him. Angela . . . '

Angela said nothing, and Celia

turned round, her eyes ablaze with triumph.

'Now perhaps you'll believe me,' she cried, 'or even believe Aunt Caroline. Stuart and Angela have been milking them for years, getting into debt in Canada, and almost being arrested for non-payment of bills, until the family helped them out. And where did it go? On bridge parties, Angela? Clothes? Silly entertaining? Certainly not on the children, by what I saw when they arrived! Or on Stuart. He's soft, but he has integrity. Angela has none. Go on, tell the truth for once. Who was driving the car when you had that accident, for instance . . . and why wasn't it insured? You had to sell your pretty baubles to pay some of the bills, hadn't you, darling?'

Angela's eyes were wide and staring.

'You must have hired a detective,' she said at last.

'Why not?' laughed Celia. 'It's time someone spiked your guns.'

The colour was returning to Angela's

face, and she looked at Celia, her eyes glittering with sudden anger.

'You've always had it in for me, haven't you?' she asked. 'Ever since I took Stuart from you. Maybe I have been a poor wife to him, but you'd have been a sight worse. You're . . . you're underhand, and mean and spiteful.'

'I'm honest,' returned Celia. 'I'm at least honest. You two are just a couple of parasites.'

Her withering glance included Lucy, who was looking at Angela unbelievingly. The gentleness which she thought was a basis of Angela's character seemed to have gone entirely. She was answering Celia back, spitefully, and made no denial of the fact that she and Stuart had been living off the Carricks for years. And what about those pathetic letters to her, and her own efforts to send help to Angela? Yet deep down she knew she ought not to be surprised. She'd been turning a blind eye to Angela's faults, when her common sense should have told her, long ago, what her sister was really like.

She stared white-faced at her sister, feeling soiled and unclean. Celia was right, in a way. How could she remain here, under the Carricks' roof, knowing that her sister owed them so much? She felt just like a . . . a parasite.

'I think you're well enough to look after the boys now, Angela,' she said, her lips stiff. 'I hope, Mrs Carrick, that you will release me from your employment. I . . . I should rather like to get on with my own affairs now.'

Mrs Carrick had said little, but now she turned to Celia.

'Please leave us now, Celia,' she said quietly.

The older girl was suddenly subdued.

'I'm sorry, Aunt Caroline. I know your views, and . . . and your reasons for keeping quiet. You're considering the children. But it galled me to see her here . . . '

'Very well. Thank you, Celia. Good evening, my dear.'

Celia swept out, and Angela turned

with a small laugh to Lucy.

'She gets all het up,' she said, with a touch of bravado. 'Surely you can't be serious, Lucy. You know you're needed here. Anyway, Stuart and I have turned over a new leaf. Mrs Carrick will tell you how sorry we are, and what we're doing.'

'I don't want to know,' cried Lucy. 'I . . . I'm so ashamed, I feel I can't look anyone in the face again. How could you, Angela!'

'We were young and silly, and in love,' mumbled Angela. 'Some people are human, you know.'

'Most people are silly when they're young,' said Lucy, her blue eyes flashing. 'But their integrity doesn't allow them to . . . to . . . steal . . . ' Her voice shook. 'I'll pack my case, Mrs Carrick,' she said quietly. 'Angela can start paying back by taking over my job. She's well enough to tackle it now.'

She went over and took the old lady's hand.

'I can't tell you how sorry I am . . . how I feel, and how wonderful you and . . . and Fergus have been. I can only say I'm sorry for some of the things I've said to you in the past.'

'Where are you going now, dear?' asked Mrs Carrick anxiously, and Lucy smiled reassuringly.

'Only to Nanny Campbell's,' she said. 'I'll be O.K., but I'd like to get on with my own life now. I . . . I don't think my sister needs me any more, and I'd like to leave now.'

Half an hour later she went out into the warmth of the summer evening to a waiting taxi. Having the taxi take her to Nanny Campbell's was an extravagance, but she didn't care. She only wanted to be in the shelter of Nanny's warm love again because she felt cold and chilled inside.

Fergus hadn't arrived home before she left, and she knew she would never see him again. The hurt of that would come later, but for the moment, Angela's tearful face could do nothing to melt her, nor her repeated assurances that she and Stuart had new plans, and would pay back every penny.

When the taxi drew up outside Nanny's cottage, she almost groped her way out, grossly over-paying the driver. A moment later she was sobbing in Nanny's arms.

★ ★ ★

Lucy returned to London the following morning by the early morning train. Nanny Campbell had wanted her to stay a few days at Airlie, but she felt she had to get away from Newton Stephens as quickly as possible.

'I'm sorry, Nanny,' she said apologetically. 'I'd rather not. I want to get away from . . . from everything. I'll come back soon, though, I promise.'

'Your heart's maybe sore just now, Miss Lucy,' Nanny told her, 'but it'll soon mend. What you need is a nice home of your own, then you'd find real happiness.'

'Yes, Nanny,' said Lucy automatically, shutting her case.

There wasn't much hope of that, she thought, dismally, with her heart already given. She'd never be able to fall in and out of love easily.

'And don't think too badly of Miss Angela,' said Nanny, then sighed deeply. 'In fact, I'm feeling it just as much as you, because I'm maybe to blame more than anybody for the silly things she's done. Your mother and I should never have spoiled her when she was wee . . . like I told you before. She did stupid, selfish things even then, but she used to come to her senses sooner or later, and try to make up for the ills she'd done. She's no' a bad lassie, just thoughtless.'

Lucy nodded soberly. Perhaps she had no right to sit in judgement on Angela, but six years of lies and deceit could hardly be wiped out in a moment.

'Maybe I'll try to see her again in a week or two, Nanny,' she promised, 'but not just yet. I just want to get myself another job, and try to find myself again. At the moment I feel so confused, Nanny, I can't see straight. I'll send you my address, but please don't give it to anyone, will you?'

The old woman glanced at her sideways.

'Not even Dr Martin?'

'Especially not Dr Martin,' said Lucy, firmly. 'I'm afraid your match-making is away off the mark. I'm not in love with Martin, or ever likely to be.'

The old woman couldn't doubt the sincerity in her voice.

'Och well, I never really thought he was the right one for you now, did I? He's a wee bit stuffy at times.'

Lucy grinned and felt better, then her eyes sobered again.

'You must let me know if Celia Grange interferes at all with your tenancy,' she insisted.

'She can't put me out,' Nanny said stoutly, 'anyway I don't think Mr

Grange would even try. I've been here far too long.'

Lucy nodded, then bent to kiss the old woman.

''Bye, Nanny. I'll write as soon as I'm fixed up.'

★ ★ ★

It wasn't so easy contacting all her friends again. Changes had been made while she was away, and she knew that her old job had been filled. She had good references, however, and soon managed to find a secretarial job to her satisfaction, though accommodation was a great deal more difficult. But at last, Ann Redding, a girl she'd known quite well, told her that a third girl was needed for the flat she shared with Madge Paull. It was better than she'd hoped, and Lucy accepted it gratefully.

She wrote, giving Nanny her address, and receiving a thankful letter in reply, saying how pleased the old woman was that she had settled down again.

A week or two later, a letter from Angela was forwarded. Lucy opened it with unsteady fingers, and read that Angela and Stuart were leaving High Crest with the twins, and that Angela was still sorry for deceiving Lucy.

'I'll make it up to you, darling, really I will,' she read.

Lucy bit her lip. She was missing them already, and longed to feel the children's small chubby arms round her neck. Angela made no mention of the other members of the family, and Lucy could well imagine that there may be wedding preparations afoot. It might even be the main reason why Angela and Stuart were getting out. Celia wouldn't want them at her wedding, yet how embarrassing it would be if they were still at High Crest.

Yet where were they going? Back to Canada? Lucy scanned the letter again. It was typical of Angela, running on in huge scrawly handwriting, but giving no real information, and almost assuming that one should know it already.

With a sigh, Lucy put the letter back in the envelope, and popped it into her handbag.

'That settles it,' said Ann Redding cheerfully from the direction of the kitchen. 'You've mooned about long enough, Lucy. You've got a date tonight to go dancing.'

'Dancing?' asked Lucy, then looked doubtful. 'Oh, Ann, I don't know . . . '

'It's the only way to get over an unhappy affair,' said Ann, 'and I speak with the voice of experience. We're going to enjoy ourselves, and Rex can soon find us another man. Madge isn't much fun now she's engaged.'

'It's not really a love affair,' protested Lucy. 'More a . . . a family matter.'

'With a man lurking around somewhere,' said Ann, briskly. 'Darling, you've got all the signs. Now come on, and get those black curls trimmed and set. It's time you looked human again.'

Lucy laughed. She was beginning to feel half human already.

It was amazing how quickly she

began to pick up the threads of her old life, she thought, as she clipped on some pretty earrings shaped like daisies, then she seemed to hear Fergus telling her she looked like a snowdrop, and knew that she had become almost two people.

'I'm only half here,' she thought, seeing the blue shadows under her eyes. 'The other half is still at High Crest.'

Yet it was good fun to go out with Ann and Rex. Sam, the large young man whom Rex had brought along, was full of boyish good humour, and made her laugh. Lucy caught Ann smiling at her approvingly, and was very grateful.

But one evening she had a headache, and asked the others to excuse her early.

'Don't break up the party, please,' she pleaded. 'I'll just get a taxi home, and have an early night.'

'Well, if you're sure . . . ' said Ann, then nodded. She'd held Lucy's hand long enough. Now she could manage her own affairs quite capably. 'All right, love,' she agreed. 'You can have some of my Ovaltine.'

Lucy paid off the taxi and began to climb the stairs. Her pretty blue cocktail dress rustled about her knees, and she wrapped her cobwebby stole round her shoulders, then fumbled in her bag for her key, as she rounded the stairs.

'About time, too,' said a voice, and she had to put out a hand to steady herself, as Fergus rose from a sitting position with his back against their door.

'I'm completely stiff,' he complained. 'I thought you were never coming home.'

Lucy was trying hard to find her voice.

'What are you doing here?' she croaked.

'I wonder that myself,' he told her dryly, taking in her evening clothes. 'It *does* look rather as though I'm wasting my time, after repeated visits to your Nanny, too. I practically had to wring this address out of her, and eventually only succeeded after I'd put all my cards on the table.'

'What cards?' asked Lucy.

She led him into the flat, and bent to light the gas fire.

'What cards?' she repeated.

'Is it true you don't love Steele?' he asked her, in a carefully casual voice. 'That you aren't going to marry him?'

'Who told you that?' she asked.

'Nanny.'

Lucy bit her lip, wondering what he'd said to Nanny to make her betray a confidence.

'Please tell me,' said Fergus. 'It's very important, Lucy.'

'It's true,' she said quietly. 'I've never been in love with Martin. But how did you manage to get Nanny to tell you all this? She's usually as close as an oyster.'

Fergus seemed suddenly nervous as he dived his hand into his pocket, and came out with a small piece of tissue paper, which he undid fumblingly.

'I showed her this,' he said shyly, and

produced a beautiful diamond and ruby ring in a Victorian setting. 'It's a betrothal ring, and has been worn by my mother and grandmother. It would have been Angela's . . . in other circumstances. I . . . I'd hoped you'd wear it, too, Lucy.'

'But . . . but Celia . . . ' she began, bewildered. 'What about Celia? You're engaged to her!'

Fergus caught her to him.

'Of course I'm not,' he told her. 'We felt we owed Celia something when Stuart walked out on her, and perhaps she was encouraged to think she was a more important part of the family than was the case. Anyway, she blackmailed you, and Mother was furious. I don't think we'll see much of Celia again!'

Suddenly Lucy found herself in a bearlike hug, which left her breathless, and Fergus was kissing her as though he meant business.

'There! Does that convince you, or do I get scratched again?'

She shook her head, and he kissed her again.

'Oh, Lucy, I've missed you so,' he told her, and ran a gentle hand over her face, playfully tweaking her small nose. 'Here, try on the ring.' He slipped it on to her third finger, where it twirled round loosely. 'Damn! We'll have to get it altered.'

But Lucy was still looking at him with troubled eyes.

'I . . . I don't know that I can wear it, Fergus,' she said, slowly. 'I'm still Angela's sister, you know, and I can't ever forget what she did.'

Fergus nodded seriously.

'She and Stuart were equally irresponsible,' he admitted, 'but they were very young and immature, and anyway, it's all in the past. They're happily settled in Edinburgh.'

'Edinburgh?' echoed Lucy.

'Yes. Didn't she tell you?'

She shook her head.

'She said she was writing. Those business trips of mine were mainly to open up another branch of the firm in Edinburgh. Stuart and Angela are going to manage the shop between them, and one day they may be able to buy me out. Angela wants to pay back what they've already borrowed, too. I think they'll manage to make a go of things, though they're sure to have a few headaches to begin with. But Stuart really loves Carrick's, and I think his experiences in Canada have toughened him.'

'I'm glad,' said Lucy, then looked doubtful again.

'And . . . and your mother?'

'Waiting to welcome you, darling. Surely you knew you had Mother eating out of your hand, as well as me. She admired you for sticking up for Angela, even if you were a bit misguided. She admires family loyalty. Anyway, Lucy darling, will you marry me and come to High Crest? I love you so much, and the old house is like a shell without you.'

'Yes, please, Fergus,' said Lucy

obediently, and only slipped out of his arms, with flushed cheeks, when Ann came home.

'Ann, this is my fiancé, Fergus Carrick,' she introduced, her voice ringing with pride. 'Ann Redding, Fergus, who has been very, very kind to me.'

'How do you do,' said Ann. 'Darling, if you need a bridesmaid, I'm practically an expert now!'

THE END

Mary Cummins also writes under the
pseudonym of Jane Carrick
and Mary Jane Warmington

We do████████ave enjoyed
read███████nt book.

Did y██████f our titles
are a█████chase?

We publis████nge of high
quality large print books including:
**Romances, Mysteries, Classics
General Fiction
Non Fiction and Westerns**

Special interest titles available in
large print are:
**The Little Oxford Dictionary
Music Book, Song Book
Hymn Book, Service Book**

Also available from us courtesy of
Oxford University Press:
**Young Readers' Dictionary
(large print edition)
Young Readers' Thesaurus
(large print edition)**

For further information or a free
brochure, please contact us at:
**Ulverscroft Large Print Books Ltd.,
The Green, Bradgate Road, Anstey,
Leicester, LE7 7FU, England.
Tel:** (00 44) **0116 236 4325**
Fax: (00 44) **0116 234 0205**

CONV IEART

Lynne C lins

They called Romily the Snow Queen, but once she had been all fire and passion, kindled into loving by a man's kiss and sure it would last a lifetime. She still believed it would, for her. It had lasted only a few months for the man who had stormed into her heart. After Greg, how could she trust any man again? So was it likely that surgeon Jake Conway could pierce the icy armour that the lovely ward sister had wrapped about her emotions?